PRAISE FOR **Nikki Loftin's** *Nightingale's Nest*:

"Unusual, finely crafted story of loss, betrayal, and healing."
★*Kirkus Reviews*, starred review

"Magical realism meets coming of age in this sensitive
and haunting novel. . . . Read this aloud and have both boys
and girls alike utterly enraptured."
★*BCCB*, starred review

"Smart and beautiful by turns . . . Once you've read it,
you'll have a hard time getting it out of your head."
—Elizabeth Bird, *School Library Journal* Blog

"It is Loftin's skill in depicting both the human
and the arboreal characters that will engage and inspire
readers. The lyrical, descriptive prose and the hopeful
ending will linger long after the final chapter."
—*School Library Journal*

"Riveting . . . This is a book you'll long remember."
—Lynda Mullaly Hunt, author of *One for the Murphys*

"An extraordinary read—I had to tear myself away from it."
—Katherine Catmull, author of *Summer and Bird*

"Perfectly captures the challenges of growing up and
dealing with loss. Get ready to have your heart touched."
—Shannon Messenger, author of *Keeper of the Lost Cities*

wish girl

wish girl

Nikki Loftin

razOr
bill

An imprint of Penguin Group USA

A division of Penguin Young Readers Group
Published by the Penguin Group
Penguin Group (USA) LLC
345 Hudson Street
New York, New York 10014

USA / Canada / UK / Ireland / Australia / New Zealand / India / South Africa / China
Penguin.com

A Penguin Random House Company

Library of Congress Cataloging-in-Publication Data

Loftin, Nikki.
Wish girl / by Nikki Loftin.
260 pages
Summary: Twelve-year-old Peter has never felt at home with his noisy family, but begins to find the strength to live and to be himself when he discovers a special valley in the Texas Hill Country and meets Annie, a girl dying of cancer who knows and accepts him from the start.
ISBN 978-1-59514-686-1 (hardcover)
[1. Individuality--Fiction. 2. Best friends--Fiction. 3. Friendship--Fiction. 4. Family problems--Fiction. 5. Cancer--Fiction. 6. Family life--Texas--Fiction. 7. Texas--Fiction.] I. Title.
PZ7.L8269Wis 2015
[Fic]--dc23
2014031004

Printed in the United States of America

1 3 5 7 9 10 8 6 4 2

For Mom

If we had a keen vision and feeling
of all ordinary human life,
it would be like hearing the grass grow
and the squirrel's heart beat,
and we should die of that roar
which lies on the other side of silence.

~George Eliot

Chapter 1

The summer before I turned thirteen, I held so still it almost killed me.

I'd always been quiet. I'd even practiced it: holding my breath, holding even my thoughts still. It was the one thing I could do better than anyone else, but I guess it made me seem weird. I got tired of my family saying, "What's wrong with Peter?"

There was a lot wrong with me. But at that moment the most serious thing was the rattlesnake on my feet.

I'd just run away from home for the first time. *Possibly the last time, too,* I thought, staring down at the ground, blinking slowly, as if I could close my eyes and make the snake vanish.

I stood as still as I could on the edge of a limestone cliff, the toes of my tennis shoes hanging off the hillside, my heartbeat thudding hard and fast at the base of my throat, my neck stiff, and my eyes on my shoes. On the diamondback rattler, gleaming brown and black and silver-gray, curled around both my feet, looped across the tops of my laces.

Its head was unmistakably wedge-shaped, and its tail was light brown, decorated with eight rattles. I'd had time to count them; I'd been standing there for at least fifteen minutes, trying not to move a single muscle.

My mouth had gone bone dry. I swallowed hard, and the snake's head, which had rested on the top of my left sneaker near my bare ankle, bobbed up, black tongue tasting the air.

I held my breath.

For a moment, I thought of kicking the snake off my feet, running for it. Then I realized it was completely wrapped around my ankles. If I tried to kick it, it would bite me for sure. So far, it was just . . . smelling me, it seemed like. I remembered that from reading about snakes when I was little. They smelled with their tongues.

I hoped it liked what it smelled, because I remembered something else. Rattlesnakes could strike at twice the length of their bodies. So this one, if it wanted to, could bite somewhere close to my throat.

Boots. I should have worn boots. Or at least jeans, instead of my stupid gym shorts from sixth-grade PE.

Dark spots swam before my eyes. I had to breathe. I did so, slowly, trying as hard as I could not to make any sound at all, not to attract the snake's attention any more than I had.

The snake didn't strike, or move, just continued to lick the air. And then, a centimeter at a time, it laid down on my feet.

Like it was planning to take a nap.

I breathed slow and easy, or tried to, and wondered how long a snake's nap might take. How long was I going to be standing there, with a snake wrapped around my ankles, waiting to be bitten or to fall over?

Someone would come looking for me, I thought. I wasn't hiding or anything. They'd find me. If someone came over the hill and ran in the same direction I had for twenty minutes or so.

Out here in the totally uninhabited countryside.

I almost laughed. That was never going to happen. I was stuck out here, with nothing to do but wait, nothing to feel but fear.

As I stood there, trying as hard as I could not to rock back and forth for balance, I felt my shoulders begin to relax. There was nothing I could do, right?

Nothing but be still. Or die.

Chapter 2

I didn't die. I didn't even get in trouble when I got home four hours later. Turns out, it's not running away when no one notices you're gone.

"What did you do today, Peter?" Dad asked, passing me the mashed potatoes at dinner. "You didn't stay in your room again, did you, buddy? You know, some fresh air would do you good."

I didn't answer for a minute. What could I tell him? "Dad, I ran away and spent the afternoon trapped by a venomous snake"? Maybe he'd feel guilty. He'd been the reason I'd left, after all. Well, his drumming anyway.

Dad had lost his job and most of his hair in the past year, and he'd decided to relive his youth or something by playing the drums. He was "brushing up his chops" to audition for a band in Austin, he said.

That afternoon, he'd tried to get me to join in, handing me

cowbells and triangles and nodding at me when I was supposed to bang on them. Father-and-son time.

I had told him the sounds gave me a headache.

I wasn't lying.

"You're so sensitive, Peter," Dad had said, disappointed in me, as usual. "You've got to toughen up."

I'd only heard that a thousand times. But for some reason, that day the truth had hit me. I'd never be tough enough for him.

I wondered if he'd believe I was tougher than a rattlesnake. I glanced up. Nope. He was wearing his perpetual "Why is my son such a weirdo?" expression. So I just answered, "I went walking."

"Oh?" Mom perked up and looked away from her lap, where she'd been typing something on her phone under the tablecloth. Probably trying to get on Facebook, even though it was practically impossible to get reception way out here. "Where did you go? Did you meet anyone?"

I thought of the snake and smiled a little. I didn't think that was what she meant.

My older sister, Laura, stopped spooning baby food into Carlie's mouth—or mostly onto her shirt and bib, as Carlie was sort of a moving target—and interrupted. "Are you kidding? Of course he didn't see anyone. Come on, Mom. You moved us out to the butt end of nowhere. There aren't any people for, like, fifty miles around."

"Laura, that negative attitude has to go," Mom argued. "I'll have you know, there are two boys Peter's age who live at a house only a mile away. This is a great place for us. It doesn't take any longer for me to commute in to the office, since there's almost no traffic—"

"Because no people," Laura interrupted, leaning back in her chair and angrily popping pieces of okra into her mouth. "No civilization," she growled through a mouth full of okra guts.

"No tattooed boyfriends," Dad added. "No potheads." He winked at me. I tried not to smile. I was the only one who'd heard, since Mom had started up again.

"Well, you're hardly one to talk about being civilized, Laura Elizabeth Stone." Mom raised her eyebrows. "Eating with your fingers? When you two go back to school this fall, I think you'll want to act a little nicer—"

That set Laura off again, on her favorite topic of having to attend a country high school where the biggest summer event was a rodeo, and 80 percent of the kids raised goats and steers for 4-H.

It was really different out here in the hill country, that was for sure. Different from our apartment in San Antonio, where we'd lived for almost eleven years. We'd only been in the new house for a week, but I could tell it wouldn't ever be home. There was nothing homey about it: a two-story, thirty-year-old wood-frame box with three different colors of vinyl siding and windows so loose they rattled in a stiff breeze.

I hated it. I think we all did. But we hadn't had much choice. Our old landlord had said that Dad's drums and guitars were driving away his other tenants. "Driving them crazy," he'd moaned the day he delivered the news that he wouldn't renew our lease.

I couldn't blame him. The noise of my family was unreal. The TV was on all the time, turned up loud enough to cover Carlie's constant tantrums and crying. My mom talked on the phone whenever she was home, or talked *at* the girls and me. When she didn't think we were listening to her—which was pretty much always—she just talked louder.

Like she was doing now, arguing with Laura. My head started to feel like something was squeezing it slowly, but hard. Carlie went from spitting food on her tray to crying. I picked at my meat loaf and thought of the valley I'd found that day. Where I'd met the snake.

It wasn't that far. Just across some fields of weeds, cacti, and a few scraggly trees and bushes that had more thorns than leaves. Then over the top of the hill behind that, past the fence made of railroad ties stacked diagonally on each other like enormous Lincoln Logs, and across the thin stretch of asphalt that was being retaken by grasses and wildflowers on both edges.

Just far enough away that I couldn't hear crying or yelling or drumming.

It had seemed like a dream. For the first time in years, I hadn't heard cars or trains, TVs or video games or people. Hadn't seen a roofline or even a plane in the sky.

I'd been alone for the first time in my whole life, almost. I liked it.

No, I loved it. Out there, my heartbeat was as loud as anything in the world.

Carlie shrieked. My head was the only thing pounding now. Well, that and Carlie's feet on the bottom of the table.

"Well, why couldn't we get a better house at least? One with high-speed Internet?" Laura asked. "It's like living on Mars."

"True," Dad agreed around a mouthful of salad. "That part's such a drag. Maybe we could get the cable company to hook us up—"

"We're on one paycheck," Mom hissed. "Mine. Did you forget?"

Dad lifted his chin in my direction, like I was supposed to say something.

I knew better.

But he didn't. He rolled his eyes—at Mom. "Like you would let me for one minute. Nag, nag, nag."

I held still. Laura did, too. Even Carlie paused in her tantrum. Then the world exploded into noise as Mom and Dad went at it, throwing blame and insults at each other as fast as they could, like they each were trying to win some invisible food fight.

And they didn't care who got hit.

"You chose this place without even consulting me, Maxine," Dad yelled. "Just because I'm out of a job doesn't mean I'm out of the family." His next word was a bullet. "Yet."

Carlie was crying full-out now, and Laura picked her up, humming some lullaby but never taking her eyes off Mom and Dad. She looked as scared as I felt.

Was this it? Were they splitting up?

My parents had always fought a little, usually in their room at night, after they thought us kids were asleep. But since Dad had been laid off eleven months ago—the same week Mom had gotten promoted to assistant manager at the bank—the yelling had gotten lots worse.

"You know we had to get away from the city, Joshua," Mom said, her voice low. "You know why." I felt her eyes on me, their eyes.

Maybe it *was* Dad's fault we'd been evicted. But it was my fault we'd had to move out here, away from the city they'd all loved. I knew that. Laura made sure to remind me every day.

Their stares burned into my skin.

"May I be excused?" My voice was a whisper. Too soft; no one heard.

The headache was getting worse, fast. It felt like something was splitting behind my right eye. Like my brain was under attack.

I held every bit as still as I had that afternoon, and I wished I was back at the rim of the valley.

And then, in my mind, I was.

My skin prickled. Like something was watching me. Something invisible and mysterious and vast. It seemed like the valley was waiting to see what I would do. I stayed motionless for longer than I ever had, wondering what was expected.

And then the valley took a breath.

Wind moved across the bowl, shifting trees and bushes like the land was a giant cat being petted. It moved fast, faster. It was almost here, almost to me.

Would the wind knock me over?

The hot air rushed around me, and the clatter of leaves sounded like excited whispers in my ears. Sounded almost like . . . hissing?

I smiled, remembering the rattler. I'd been so still, when it slid across my feet it had probably thought I was a tree or a rock. Thought I belonged there.

I stood for hours, snake around my ankles, fear in my throat. The breeze rose back up, pushing strands of my hair past my ears. It reminded me of when my grandma was alive, and she would stroke the hair back over my ear, feather-gentle.

The world around me came to life, like an orchestra tuning up. Somewhere to my right, a bird began to sing, a bunch of mixed-up trills. A mockingbird, I thought. Grasshoppers and frogs joined in. Something larger must have moved a little farther away, since I heard the sharp thud of rocks knocking together and sliding downhill.

The sun beat on my face, and I saw the shadows of clouds moving across the sky even with my eyes shut, as the light behind my eyelids went from red to black to red again.

Someone—something—was watching me. A shiver ran up my spine and made goose bumps prickle on my arms. It was the same feeling I used to get when my teacher would lean over my desk to tell me what a good job I'd done, in a quiet voice so no one else would hear.

Then something else sent a chill up my back. The snake was moving.

I opened my eyes and waited as it went from being wrapped around my ankles to slithering across the rocky soil toward a bush. And then, with a flick of its rattle, it slid under the bush like it had never been on my ankles at all.

I let out my breath and turned to go, my feet numb with the effort it had taken to stay in one place for so long. For a moment I wanted to shout, holler, and whoop as loud as I could. But before I did, a hawk flew by and yelled for me—screeched and wheeled right overhead, like it was saying hello. Or well done.

I waved with one hand, wondering why the hawk's answering call sounded like laughter. Why the sudden gust of wind felt like gentle hands pushing at my shoulders. Pretending to try to tip me over, the same way my grandpa used to when we'd sit on his porch in Houston, just the two of us, him telling dirty jokes and me holding back laughter so Mom and Dad wouldn't come and hear and make him stop.

Suddenly, the rattlesnake seemed like one of his jokes. Dangerous and funny and private. No one would believe me if I told them anyway.

"Helloooo?" The valley disappeared, and I blinked. Laura

was waving her hand in front of my face. I didn't know how long she'd been doing it, how long I'd been staring at my plate.

It must have been a long time. Laura looked really worried, and her voice quivered when she asked, "What's wrong with you, Peter?"

Chapter 3

"Peter?" Laura repeated, louder. She had her hand on my arm. How long had she been touching me? I hadn't even felt her. I'd been lost in my thoughts. "Were you having a seizure or something?"

Mom and Dad were still fighting, in angry whispers, but standing by the door. So we wouldn't hear? A few words came through: " . . . therapist bills or groceries? You have to try harder. He needs more help. He's still not himself. . . . "

Talking about me. I could feel the blood rushing to my face, and I shook Laura's hand away. "No. It's nothing. I was daydreaming. Just . . . leave me alone." I looked at my arm. She'd accidentally wiped some of Carlie's baby food there. "Gross, Laura." I flicked it at her.

"Fine," she said. "Be that way. Weirdo." She pulled her phone out of her pocket, waving it around to try to get a signal, ignoring us all.

I cleared my throat. "Mom, may I be excused? Mom? Mom?"

I didn't think she'd heard me, but then—"Peep!" Carlie screamed her version of my name at the top of her lungs. "Peep!"

Mom swung her head around. "Did you need something, Peter?"

"I have a headache," I said. "May I be excused?"

Mom fussed over me for a minute, tried to get me to take a Tylenol, and when I wouldn't, she stuffed a chocolate chip cookie into my hand like it was some sort of secret-recipe painkiller.

"Come watch a movie with us tonight," she said as I cleared my plate. "We're going to do a *Fast and Furious* marathon the whole weekend, to celebrate having almost all the unpacking done so soon."

"No, thanks. I'm just going to go sit in my room." Mom chewed on her lower lip; I could tell she was trying not to react. "To read, Mom. That's all."

I wasn't lying. I figured I would read up on snakes again. It might come in handy.

I left the table and had almost made it to my door when I remembered we'd put all the nature books in the living room. I was walking back when I heard Laura say softly, "What is it with Peter? Did you even notice him, just sitting there like a lump? We shouldn't have moved. He's worse than ever. Tell the truth. Is he brain-dead or something? Did you drop him on his head when he was a baby?"

"Laura Stone!" Mom's voice was harsh, but quiet, too. "Your

brother's perfectly fine. He's just . . . different. Introverted. And you know what he was going through last spring. We *had* to move, for more than one reason. So stop complaining about it. Remember, stay positive around him."

"Whatever," Laura said. "I've tried. It's not working. He's getting weirder since we moved out here. All this time alone? It's not good for . . . whatever he has."

"You know, you may be right," Dad started. "I mean, he's always been so quiet, it's hard to tell what he's thinking—or feeling. But he may actually be getting more depressed since we moved. I was wondering if . . . "

I tiptoed back to my room without the snake book, my face burning, not wanting to hear whatever my dad was saying back.

It wasn't like I was going to do anything anyway. I wasn't going to go rushing in there and defend myself. Standing up to them—to anyone—scared me more than running away, any day. Laura had told me a thousand times, and it was true: I was a wimp. I was a pushover. I was an embarrassment.

They all thought I was defective. I'd heard Mom tell Dad more than once that I'd been "born into the wrong family." I even knew what they meant; I didn't fit in with the rest of them, except maybe Carlie. When she was asleep.

But it didn't make it hurt any less.

Chapter 4

I ran away again as soon as it got light enough to see. This time, I left a note on my bed just in case Mom or Dad went so far as to open my door to check on me, and I snagged a couple of granola bars and a bottle of water to stuff in my backpack.

"Peep?" Carlie called as I ran though the living room on my way to the door. She was watching TV in her playpen, which meant Mom had already been up and gone back to sleep, I assumed. It was Saturday, after all.

Carlie had taken her diaper off and was tearing it into little bits, so I stopped for a second to gather up the pieces and toss them, then wrap another one around her. "Don't tear this one, Carlie," I whispered. "That could get messy." She put her finger up to her lips, made a shushing sound, and nodded. Then she held her arms up again. "Peep?" She wanted to come with me.

"Not today, Carbar," I answered. I put my hands together and made a hissing sound. "There's snakes out there. Lots and lots of big snakes." I pretended my hands were snake jaws, and she broke into peals of laughter. I almost stayed there with her, playing, but then I heard a door on the other side of the house squeal open, and knew I'd get stuck with babysitting and cleaning if I hung around. The normal Saturday routine.

"Bye-bye." I waved and left, my feet quiet on the carpet.

The night before, I'd gone looking for my old boots—the pair Dad had bought for me during my three-week failed Boy Scout experiment a year and a half ago. I'd found them in one of the remaining moving boxes and left them in the front hall, hidden behind Carlie's baby swing. I slipped them on right outside the door. They pinched a little bit, but I didn't care. They'd be fairly snake-proof, I hoped.

I walked faster than the day before, since I knew where I was going. Or at least where I was going to start.

The snake wasn't there this time, even though I looked at what I thought was the same bush it had crawled under. For a second I wondered if I had imagined its appearance.

No. The snake had been real, more real than most of the things in my life—video games and TV shows, comic books and chores.

I walked to the ledge I'd stopped at before and scanned the valley. It didn't feel strange like it had yesterday. I didn't get the sense anything was watching.

But something was calling me. Halfway down the hillside, where another hill pushed up against the one I was on, a line of trees, growing larger further down, gleamed bright green, their leaves waving in the morning air. I pelted down the hill, my boots slipping on limestone rocks that weren't attached to anything, the tufts of thick grasses stopping my fall before I could slip too far.

It was crazy running down the hill. I didn't care. The wind rushed up against my face as I went, promising to catch me if I stepped too far away from the ground.

The cluster of oak trees was farther away than I'd thought, and I got out of breath. I slowed down and started walking more quietly. There might be deer hiding in the trees, I thought. If I was quiet enough, maybe I'd see one.

But by the time I pushed back some smaller bushes and stepped under the oaks, I was the only thing making any sound on the hillside.

I couldn't seem to stop making noise. Every step I took in my clunky boots cracked seedpods and acorns underfoot, popping them like a bunch of Black Cat fireworks in the silence of the grove. Last fall's windblown drifts of leaves crunched and crackled underfoot, and even my breathing seemed loud and out of place.

I'd never see a deer or another snake or anything else if I kept making so much noise. I stopped, looked around, and saw a large rock jutting out from the mounds of dead leaves. No, not just a rock: a pile of them. As I approached, I realized I was following the slope of the hillside right up to the point where it touched the other hill.

When I got there, I looked down the slope. The rocks were old and weathered, covered with dried algae-like stuff and old moss. But there were damp patches underneath. What if I kept going, walked along the stones? Would I find a creek? A lake? Animals hung out near lakes, I knew that.

I slipped off my boots to stay quiet and tucked them in my backpack with my granola bars. Then, slowly, I crept down the rocks, trying to be as silent as possible.

A minute or so later, I stopped. Below me, only a few yards away, was a pool. A deer stood there, its head bowed. A doe, I thought. It didn't have antlers like the males I'd seen at the zoo. Suddenly, it jumped back from the water like something had surprised it, and it stepped nervously away from the edge. I held my breath, wondering if the doe had heard me. Its nostrils flared. Maybe it had smelled me?

Then, stepping as carefully as I had, it lifted one silent foot at a time and tiptoed away from the water's edge, slipping through the trees and back out onto the hillside. I began to move again, curious to see what was in the pool. What had startled the deer?

But when I got to the rock where it had stood drinking, I looked into the water, and nothing was there. The pool itself was beautiful, with rocks overhanging one edge, making a small cave-like hole at that end. The surface wasn't more than ten feet across, although the water looked at least five feet deep in the center. It was clean, and when the sunlight shone through the oak leaves overhead, it sparkled across the top of the pool. I sat there on the rock, staring into the water with my legs crossed and my hands folded, feeling hypnotized. After a while I closed my eyes. I hadn't slept well the night before, dreaming of snakes and valleys that came to life.

I might have dozed; I wasn't sure. But something woke me. A sound? A humming. I held still, feeling what had to be legs on me, tickling the hairs on my arms. Had ants crawled onto me? Bees? I opened my eyes, remembering the snake, making sure to move only my eyelids.

My arms were covered with dragonflies. No, they were smaller than that. But similar. Brightly colored, red and blue and glossy black, with thin graceful wings and long segmented bodies. They must have decided I was a good perch, because there were at least twenty of them on each of my arms.

They liked me. I could feel it in the way they moved, dancing on my skin. Just like the valley liked me—and for the same reason my family didn't.

Because I was still and quiet.

I'd finally found the place where I could be alone. Where I could be me. It was perfect.

I'll always be quiet here, I thought to the valley. *I promise. I'll never yell, or scream, or ruin you with a bunch of racket.*

Something tickled my hair in response, and I knew that the

dragonfly things were up there, too. I felt a laugh welling up inside me and tried to keep it from coming out. If I made a noise, or moved, they would all fly off.

But the tickling on top of my ear got to be too much, and I let out a small sound, half a sigh.

They all took flight, skimming over the water. I did laugh then.

And someone muttered, "Dang it."

Chapter 5

I jumped up, and the baby dragonflies—or whatever they were—spiraled away from the water entirely, deserting me. I whipped my head around, wondering where the voice had come from. Was the person invisible? Enough weirdness had happened in this valley that I wasn't sure anything could surprise me.

But then something moved, and I saw it—her. Sitting on the other side of the pool, half-hidden by a bush, a small face with a knitted brown hat on top, covering her hair. How had I missed her?

I said the words out loud.

"I blend," the girl said, stepping away from the bushes. She held something in her hand. A sketchpad, it looked like, and a charcoal pencil—an expensive one, I thought. It was the kind my art teacher at school used, the kind she never let the kids touch since we would "just ruin them anyway."

The girl looked about my age. She was maybe a few inches

shorter, even if I wasn't tall for being almost thirteen. Dressed all in green and brown, with her brown skin just lighter than the tree trunks around us, she did sort of blend. Until she moved.

"Who are you?" the girl asked. The insects around us had fallen quiet.

"Peter," I answered. Without warning, a wave of heat rushed through me. I recognized the feeling: anger. "Peter Stone," I repeated, trying to keep my voice calm. I never let my feelings show, not if I could help it.

I wanted to spit, though. My tongue tasted bitter all of a sudden. Like the anger was literally filling my mouth.

It figured. I had finally found a place to be alone, to be quiet, and this girl was here. Maybe she even lived nearby. She'd fill the valley with noise and talking. I turned back to the water, wishing her away.

"Apt," she said, then settled back into a cross-legged position and began to sketch. She didn't say anything else.

Apt? What had she meant by that? Curiosity itched at me worse than the baby dragonflies had. But I wasn't going to speak. If I stayed quiet enough, she'd leave. It had always worked at school, on the playground, even at home. If I stayed still, stayed boring, people left me alone.

Mostly. A shiver went down my back, remembering when that hadn't worked. Remembering what had happened to make my parents move us all so far away from home. What had made my dad look at me every day like he was ashamed.

I shook the dark thoughts away and concentrated on the girl. What was she sketching? And why had she said *apt*? I thought I knew what that meant.

Appropriate.

I couldn't stand it. I had to ask.

"What do you mean?"

She glanced up, brown eyes deeper than the pool between us. She frowned down at her sketchbook, then at me.

"Your name. Peter Stone. Also, a bit repetitive. What were your parents thinking?"

Now this girl was really starting to annoy me. Why did she think my name was apt and repetitive? I stood up.

"Don't," she called out. "I'm almost done."

"Don't what?"

"Don't move just yet," she said, motioning for me to sit back down. "I've almost got you. I wasn't able to get all the damselflies. . . . " Her voice trailed off, and I stared at her. Damselflies? Oh, that was what the little dragonflies were called. Then I got it. She'd been drawing them—and me. I settled back down, feeling strange. No one had ever drawn me. I wasn't interesting-looking. Plain brown hair, brown eyes, medium-sized. Nothing special. In fact, I was invisible to most everyone.

This girl was the kind people drew, though. She reminded me of the damselflies as she worked: Her arms were thin and . . . elegant. Her eyelashes fluttered like their lacy wings had. She looked a little like a fairy, although the expression on her face was pure human grumpiness.

"What?" I said, wondering if she'd come back with another one-word answer.

"I can't get your face right, not now. Not when you're moving, Stone Boy."

"Stone Boy?"

"Well, yes," she said, slapping her sketchpad shut and walking on her toes around the circle of rocks to where I was. She was barefoot like me. "Peter means stone, of course. Or rock. And I thought you were one, for a while. I mean, how do you do that? I've never seen anything like it."

"Do what?" I had never been so confused by a person in my life. It sounded like she was speaking English, but I wasn't following half of her words.

"Hold still," she said, reaching out and putting my hand in the air like she was posing me. "See? You don't even tremble. Amazing. You could be a surgeon with hands like that."

A shadow passed over her face then, and I looked up. Was it getting overcast? I heard the flip of pages and looked back. She was showing me her drawing.

I let out my breath in a great whoosh. It was . . . "Amazing," I echoed. "You're a real artist." She was—she'd drawn the rocks and the damselflies and me, all just exactly right. None of the parts looked too big or too small. She'd shaded the edges of things with the charcoal side of the pencil to make the shadows from the oak leaves fall in the right places. Even the fingers on my hand were perfect. Not even the art teacher at my old school could draw fingers.

"Thanks," she said, examining the picture. "I think I got your face. Faces are hard. But you kept yours so still, like a statue. It was easier than usual. Honestly, the damselflies moved more than you did. There must have been a hundred of them." She folded the sketchbook under one arm, pulled a pair of tennis shoes out of the bag she'd stashed her pencil in, and stood up to slip them on. "You're phenomenal, you know. I wasn't sure you were real at first. I'd been wishing all morning for a model. I thought maybe I'd wished you here."

She didn't sound like she was kidding. "Really?" I said after a few seconds of watching her clamber back around the rocks. "You thought you . . . wished me here?"

Maybe she'd felt what I had—that this valley was magical, somehow. Like there were things here that couldn't be explained, that didn't happen in the rest of the world.

"Sure," she said, right before she disappeared back over the rim of the pool's ledge. "I mean, I am a wish girl, right? I get what I wish for."

"What?" I called out, trying to follow her, but I stopped to grab my boots, since I knew I'd never be able to chase her barefoot over the hillside. By the time I got my boots on and ran to the spot where she'd vanished between two trees, I couldn't find her. Couldn't see her, which was strange since the hills were practically bare around us, except for the cleft that hid the pool.

I climbed a bit, up to a ledge where I had a view of everything, but I didn't see her again, even though I stayed there for ten minutes, waiting, watching. Maybe she blended in with the valley? Maybe she had hidden somewhere and was waiting for me to leave so she could climb out and go home—wherever home was. One of the two houses on this side of the hill?

Or maybe, I thought . . . maybe she was part of the magic of the valley. She'd said she was a wish girl.

I shook the thought away. I was being stupid. She wasn't anything special, just a girl. Probably she had a bunch of friends she would bring with her the next time, down into this peaceful place. Screaming girls, who'd run around the valley, exploring it, filling it with words.

Ruining it.

She'd wished for me? Huh. Well, I'd been wishing for a long time to be alone, really alone, with no one to bug me, or talk at me, or tell me what a failure I was. I thought I'd found that here.

Maybe she got what she wished for. But as for me?

She wasn't any sort of wish come true.

Chapter 6

The next day, I wished I'd never met her.

It all started when I went back to the pool. I knew I shouldn't have gone. Even though nobody seemed to have missed me at home the day before, three days of disappearing was probably stretching my luck. But the valley was a special place. And the girl had called me phenomenal. And amazing. No one had ever called me anything like that before.

When I got there, I was alone. But there were a whole bunch of bugs—water striders skating across the top of the pond and tadpoles underneath, wiggling small black teardrop bodies around the edge of the water. I watched them for a long time, certain they were moving in patterns the longer I stared, making shapes, dancing almost—before I realized the girl was back.

And she was sketching me again. "Don't move," she called out softly when I reached up to scratch an old mosquito bite on my neck. "I've almost got it."

Her voice broke the morning stillness and scared off a few of the birds that had hopped closer to me through the underbrush.

I sighed. I'd been right. She was going to turn out to be one of those noisy kids.

"Listen, wish girl," I said. I still didn't know her real name. She fixed that.

"Annie," she answered, slapping her sketchpad shut and scrambling across the rocks. She had some sort of material wrapped around her ankles, navy blue like the kind the sporty kids wore when they'd hurt themselves playing. She saw me looking and took the ankle supports off as she spoke, the sound of Velcro chasing one last sparrow away from the pool. "I'm Annie Blythe. Do you live around here?" She stuffed the wraps in her bag.

"Yeah. Unfortunately. But what I was going to say was, I wish you would—"

She didn't let me finish. "Hang out with you? Yes, I will. I could tell the first time I saw you that you could use some company. I'm intuitive that way."

I almost laughed, but I didn't want to give her the wrong idea. "No, I don't need company. I was trying to be quiet."

"Oh, were you meditating?" Annie flopped down next to me, folded her legs impossibly into a pretzel, closed her eyes, settled her hands on her knees, and began to chant. "Ommmmmm."

I'd never heard an om that loud. They could probably hear her in Tibet.

"No," I said. "I just want to be alone."

That only made her om louder.

It was no use. No matter how much I wanted to tell her to bug off, make her go, it wasn't going to work. I would have to leave. "Nice to meet you, Annie," I lied.

"Oh, come on," she said, grabbing my arm and pulling me back when I stepped away. "I'm sorry I ruined your little bug-infested interlude."

"My what?" I shook my head and shook her arm off. "Never mind. I've gotta go." I started down the rocks, wondering if there were more ponds nearer the valley floor. Ponds that didn't have annoying, noisy girls by them.

"Ouch," I heard. I looked back. Annie was leaned over, holding her head. Well, her hat. She had on the brown cap again. It made her head look like a giant acorn.

"Are you okay?" She'd fallen over; her sketch materials were scattered all around her. I sighed and headed back up to help. "What happened? Did you hit your head?"

"No," she said, and I noticed her eyes were crinkled around the edges and her lips were drawn tight.

"Did you trip? Maybe you need to put those ankle wraps back on."

"My ankles are fine, really," she whispered, pushing herself up and rocking back and forth on the balls of her feet slightly. "It's my head."

"What's wrong?"

"Nothing. Just a headache. I get them."

"Me too."

"Oh?" Annie managed after a few seconds. I could tell talking really hurt, though. "Why do you get headaches?"

"Noise," I said. "Constant noise." I thought of Carlie and Laura and Mom. "Mostly noisy girls."

Annie smiled a little, but only for a second. "Here, try this," I said and grabbed her hand. There was a spot my mom had showed me once, in between the thumb and pointer finger, on the web part of the hand. If you pinched it just right, for long enough, sometimes the headaches would go away.

"It's not working," Annie said, watching me rub her hand. Probably thinking I was weird. "This isn't the acupressure-fixing kind of headache anyway. But thanks for trying."

"Oh, sorry." I let her hand drop. "Well, my dad always says, nobody ever died of a headache."

Annie burst out laughing, holding her head at the same time, like each laugh was a knife through her brain.

What had I said?

After a few seconds, she stood up, put the art supplies I'd handed her in her bag, and said, "Let's go then. Where are we going, by the way?"

I sighed. How did I put this? *No offense, but I sort of want to be by myself. Can you find somewhere else to go? Like the North Pole?*

No, that would be rude. An argument would be way worse than just leaving. I had a thought as I started back down the hill. "Are you out here alone?"

"Are you?" she shot back, following me across the rocks.

"Yeah," I said. "So you live around here? Which house?"

"I don't live here. I live near Houston. I'm going to camp over the hill at Doublecreek Farm."

"There's a camp near here?" I couldn't remember seeing anything as big as a camp.

"Well, it's a small camp. Only twenty kids. It starts tomorrow." She didn't seem excited.

"How long is it?" How long was she going to be hanging around the valley, I meant.

"Two weeks." She sounded miserable.

"That's short. Do you miss your mom or something?"

"I wish." Annie rolled her eyes. "She came along."

I couldn't help smiling. "Seriously?" I thought the whole point of camp was for kids to get independent. Although that didn't seem to be a problem for her.

"Well, only for the weekend," Annie said. "She'll drive back to Houston Sunday night."

"Doesn't she care that you're just . . . wandering around?" I wondered if I should tell her about the rattler. Maybe that would scare her off.

"No. I mean, she didn't yesterday. But I told her I met a friend, an older kid, and we were hanging out. I hope that was okay."

She'd told her mom about me? "Older? I'm only twelve. Well, almost thirteen. How old are you?"

"Twelve. So?"

"So, you lied. We're the same age."

Annie shrugged. "No big. Age is just a number. I think I read that on a birthday card."

"So she was okay with you being gone all the time?"

"Yeah, she'd pretty much let me do anything I asked for." She paused, and her lips got tight. "Well, almost anything."

"Even hang out with some older boy she's never met? I guess she *will* let you do anything."

"Well, she made me take my phone for emergencies. Of course, she probably doesn't realize you can't get any signal out here. Oh, and also I told her you were a girl."

"A girl?"

"A Girl Scout, in fact." She skipped ahead of me while I sputtered. "Named Jasmine Penelope."

"Wait, what? Why'd you say that?" I chased after her. She was fast, and she moved almost silently over the rocks. "Why Jasmine Penelope?" Did she think I looked like a Jasmine Penelope? It sounded like a brand of potpourri.

"Well, what was I supposed to say? 'Mom, I'm going to go hang out in the countryside with some stranger boy I met yesterday? And yes, he's probably an ax murderer?' Trust me, she was much happier with the Girl Scout story."

I could see her point. "Good call." I hesitated. The rocks had gotten flatter and fewer, and she had started moving through brush. Poison-ivy-looking brush. "Um, where are we going?"

"To the bottom of the valley, of course," she said. "I figure we'll find a stream or something. Keep up, will you? I'm going to see if I can get a sketch of you covered with leeches or bees or wasps or something. I wonder how many scorpions live down there."

"What?"

I thought she was kidding. I hoped she was. I followed anyway, waving mosquitoes away from my face, listening to her hum "The Bear Went over the Mountain," wondering where my quiet day had gone. Wishing Annie hadn't come along. She was nice, I guessed. But weird and bossy. And a liar. For all I knew, she really was planning to sketch me covered in fire ants or something. And even though it had been cool to be drawn the first time, it had gotten old fast. I hadn't come out here to be watched or studied. I'd come out to . . . well, to see what I could see, just like Annie was humming.

I wasn't going to see anything with her making all that racket.

But then, when we reached the bottom of the valley and found the waterfall, we both stopped in our tracks. The waterfall glittered and shone like a cascade of diamonds and sapphires, singing against the stones as it fell, thrumming against the ground so that I could feel it in my feet.

It was stunning. Even Annie got as quiet as I was, quieter than she'd ever been. I think that was the only reason we were able to hear the gunshots over the sound of the falling water.

Chapter 7

"What was that?" Annie reminded me of Carlie in a thunderstorm, scared, chewing on her lower lip. I just hoped she wasn't going to freak out.

"Guns," I said. "Someone's shooting."

In San Antonio, I'd heard gunshots a few times. There, it meant someone was getting shot at. I didn't think it meant that out here. "They're probably hunting," I whispered. The shots had come from up the hill, in the direction we'd been walking, maybe a little to the left.

"For what?" Annie said, the sass back in her voice. "Deer? Dove? It's June. This is nothing-at-all season, Peter."

"Target practice?" I tried. I started walking again, in the opposite direction of the gunfire. It was strange: As I walked I noticed all the mosquitoes and even some wasps flying as fast as they could up the hill. Flying toward the shooting, like they were late to something.

"No one lives here," she said. "This entire valley belongs to the Colonel's wife."

I swear, I spent the whole time with Annie wishing she'd go away or wondering what she was talking about.

"Who? What colonel?"

"A dead one," Annie said, examining the waterfall. Once I looked at it closer, I realized it might not have qualified as a real waterfall. It was only about three feet tall, and it fell into a streambed that couldn't have been more than knee-deep. There was a steep stone cliff on one side, and the water seemed to come from someplace right above the fall that I couldn't see. Maybe there was some sort of spring. The rock was all limestone around here, and I knew from science class that meant caves and underground streams.

The trees on the sides of the stream were oaks, but I could see a few small cypresses with their roots stuck in the water like skinny brown legs.

"A dead colonel," I repeated, following Annie as she crept to the top of the fall on slick rocks. She slipped once. I almost reached out to catch her, but she gave me a look that said *hands off*. Oh, well. If she slipped and fell, it was her fault.

"Yeah, a dead colonel," Annie said eventually, once she'd climbed over a bunch of branches, scaring up a cloud of gray moths that had been resting there. "Mom said I couldn't run around here unless it was okay with the Colonel's wife. Mom went by yesterday morning." She stopped. "Didn't you get permission?"

"Um, no," I said. Was it my imagination, or did the moths land on the trunk of an oak tree in a pattern that looked a lot like an old man's face?

"You didn't get permission?"

I shook my head. "I didn't know this land belonged to anyone."

"You dirty little trespasser," Annie crowed. "I can't believe you didn't get caught."

"You said the Colonel's wife owns it?" I said, feeling slightly nervous. Colonels were military. She probably had a lot of guns. "Do you think that was her shooting? Maybe I'd better go." I didn't like the idea of being shot as a trespasser down here, miles away from a hospital.

"Nah, she wouldn't shoot you. She's crazy, but not murderously crazy."

"Then crazy how? By the way, that's not very nice." The kids at my last school had called me crazy, too, just because I didn't like to do the things they did. They thought anyone who didn't run around screaming and playing football was an idiot, I guess.

Annie stopped, climbed on top of the biggest branch she found, and sat there, swinging her legs.

"Well, don't blame me. My mom's the one who said she was crazy."

"Why?" I climbed up next to her. We had a great view of the whole streambed from here. I let my legs swing, too.

"The Colonel's wife said something about how I could come down here if the valley would let me. Like it wasn't her decision. It was the land's." She laughed. "Weird, huh?"

"Okay, slightly crazy." I remembered, though, the feeling from the day before. Like I was being tested. I wondered, if I had moved—if I hadn't stayed quiet—would the valley have done something to make me leave?

Would the snake have bitten me?

Maybe the Colonel's wife wasn't all that nuts. But I wasn't about to say so to Annie.

"I don't care one way or the other, just so long as I can run around down here. It's so beautiful. It inspires me." She smiled again, a weird little twist of her mouth that didn't look particularly happy. "Anyway, she wasn't exactly going to say no, was she?"

My mind spun. *No* was pretty much a mom's favorite word, in my experience. "Why not?"

"Well, you know. I am a wish girl. That's what I'm doing here. Going to camp. It's my wish."

"Your wish?" I almost laughed. I swear, this girl was as crazy as they come. "I can't even understand half of what you're saying. Are you sure your brain is all there?"

The smile dropped off her face. "Well, for now," she whispered. Her voice was stripped bare of all the laughter.

I turned to face her, but she wouldn't look at me. She was tracing the line a termite or something had made on the branch, a crazy, looping half tunnel that meandered through the bark.

"What did I say?"

"I told you I was a wish girl," she said. "Get it?"

"Um, no," I said. A wish girl? I thought she'd just been joking around. What did she mean? From the sound of it, nothing good. "Like wishes that come true?"

She hopped down, agitated, and started back along the side of the stream, her strides stirring up dead leaves and dust.

"No," I heard her say, even though she wasn't speaking loudly for the first time all day. "The kind that don't."

Chapter 8

I could tell Annie didn't want to talk anymore. And I was sort of glad. Because when we got a little farther down the stream, we found the most beautiful place I'd ever seen, and words would have spoiled it for sure.

I almost slammed into her coming around the last bend. The trees had thinned out, but there was a bunch of brush and a huge red oak right at the corner, and when she'd gone around the turn, she'd stopped stock-still in the middle of the narrow path.

I could see why.

Ahead of us, stretching for hundreds of yards, was a wild-flower field. It was red and yellow and orange, all black-eyed Susans, firewheels, and Indian paintbrushes. I took a deep breath and smelled air thick with pollen and nectar.

The sound of the waterfall had died off, and now what I heard was bees. Thousands of bees, humming and buzzing over the field. Grasshoppers, too, I saw, as Annie stepped carefully into the middle of the field, and the long-legged insects flew away to both sides.

Annie said what I was thinking. "I wish I could stay here forever." She went to the very center of the field and sat down right in the flowers. I could barely see her head, the small brown cap over the tops of the wildflowers looking like a giant Mexican hat flower poking up. Then she reached up and pulled her hat off.

What in the world? Her hair was red. Not red like normal red hair—hers was dyed red, the color of fire trucks and ambulances and stop signs.

I couldn't help making a sound then. I laughed out loud, in surprise. Annie shot me a look. "You got a problem?"

"No," I said, making my way through the flowers to sit next to her. She looked like an enormous Indian paintbrush. "It's just, I've never seen a girl with hair that color. Except on TV. Your mom must be cool."

"I told you, my mom lets me do whatever I want." She closed her eyes again.

Spoiled, I thought. "I bet you don't even wash the dishes."

"So?" she replied, eyes still shut. "Why would you wash dishes when you could be making art? Do you think Frida Kahlo spent her days leaning over a sink full of soapy water? Do you think Andy Goldsworthy spends all his time doing the laundry?"

I didn't answer. I felt pretty stupid. I mean, I'd heard of Frida

Kahlo—she was the Mexican painter with the unibrow. We'd studied her in art, and I liked her paintings because there was usually a monkey in them.

A deep sigh came from Annie. "Go ahead," she said. "Ask."

Fine. "I know Frida Kahlo. Who's Andy Goldsworthy?"

"Oh my gosh," Annie said, suddenly bubbling up with excitement. "Only the coolest nature artist in the world. I went to New York City when I was eight for my first wish, and I got to go out to this sculpture park. Andy Goldsworthy had taken the things that were there—stones, wood, all sorts of stuff—and used them to make art out of nature. It was . . . amazing."

I didn't get it. He took sticks and rocks and made art? I shook my head. "How can you improve on something like this?" I waved a hand at the flower field.

"You don't get it," Annie said. "I mean, I'm not sure you can, unless you've at least watched his videos or seen one of his books. I wish I had my books here with me. I would show you art like you never imagined—I have books about all sorts of artists, modern ones and the old masters, too."

I smiled. She was this excited about art? I wondered out loud, "Planning to grow up to be an artist, huh?"

"I'm not going to wait until I grow up," she whispered. "I'm going to do it now. I have to." She stopped talking and looked around, her gaze flashing like a hummingbird from flowers to sky to tree limbs. I glanced around, too, wondering what she was looking for.

"I *will* do it. Now. This week!"

"Do what?"

She didn't answer, just kept talking to herself. "I'll have to think about it," she said at last. "It's tricky. The hill country has a rather limited palette. . . . "

I settled back in the grass, wondering what she was going on about. Whatever it was, it seemed to have cheered her up. Or distracted her, at least. She paced around the clearing, muttering and picking up small things from the ground—leaves, sticks? I couldn't tell. I lay slowly back on the grass, sending a silent apology to any ants or beetles who might still be in the danger zone. I didn't want to hurt anything in this beautiful place, not even accidentally.

I'm sure I squished a few ants, though. I couldn't help it; there were hundreds of them on the ground, all around me. I fed one of them a tiny crumb of the granola bar I was gnawing. It was strange: The ants weren't crawling on me like they usually did. They came up to my legs or arms, felt at me with their antennas, and then went around. Like they were giving me personal space.

So weird.

Weirder was the way the birds flew. I'd been staring at the sky, trying to ignore Annie and her frustrated sounds as she searched for whatever. If a bird flew overhead, I would trace its path with my finger, following the shapes of its flight. Then I thought about designing new paths—how I would fly if I could be a bird, just for a moment—all loops and inclines and steep descents. I started drawing imaginary trails overhead, slowly, my finger moving carefully—and then, a few seconds later, maybe a minute, I swear, a bird would start across the sky, echoing the exact path I'd sketched.

Not close to the pattern, but exactly on it.

At first I figured it was a fluke. But after the third swallow—or sparrow, I couldn't tell at this distance—flew directly along my course, I sat up. Was I imagining it?

One way to tell. I got more creative, drawing imaginary curlicues and spirals, even letters—*Annie*—in cursive. I held my eyes open wide, to make sure I wasn't falling asleep, dreaming the whole thing.

And then a bird—a scissortail, I think—came along not thirty seconds later and followed the track like it was being pulled by a magnet.

Unreal. Magic. The wind ruffled my hair like it had the day before, and I whispered, "Cool. Thanks."

I had to show Annie this.

But when I stood up, she was gone.

Dang it. I never knew a girl who could disappear so quickly. She was like a grasshopper, here one second, gone the next. I scanned the meadow. With her bright red hair, she'd show up there. Maybe she'd gone back to the stream. I didn't want to call out and destroy the quiet of the valley, but I was starting to get worried. She'd had a headache, and she'd fallen . . . maybe she was sick.

I was annoyed again. Just my luck, to find the coolest place in the world but have to spend my time looking for a lost girl. But as I searched for Annie—by the stream, up the hill, around the rocks—and didn't find her, I started to feel guilty. Maybe she was really lost. Maybe hurt somewhere . . .

I hadn't examined the other side of the meadow that well. Maybe she'd fallen down into a sinkhole or something. I'd have to go back. I started calling softly as I ran. "Annie!"

I thought I heard something from a long way off—much deeper in the valley, across the meadow and through at least one more grove of trees. I ran, not paying attention to how much noise I was making. "Annie!" I called again.

And then I heard one word, clear as day but still too far: "Help!"

Chapter 9

I wasn't the fastest runner. Dad said it was because I spent too much time indoors. He could run; he'd even been the quarterback on his high school football team before he tore some tendon and had to quit.

But I might have broken an Olympic record racing toward the sound of that small "Help!"

I ran through a stand of trees faster than was safe, probably, ducking under grapevines and low limbs, jumping over rocks and small bushes.

In less than a minute, I emerged from the trees and found myself in another meadow. This one was dotted with huge boulders and didn't have any flowers in it. No colors but gray and green.

Well, except for Annie's bright red head, which poked up behind a boulder. "Help me!" she said again.

I was right, she must have gotten stuck or bitten or . . . My brain buzzed with possibilities as I raced to her side, wondering how far we were from real help, medical help.

But when I got to her, I stopped. She wasn't hurt. Wasn't stuck. She was . . . "What are you doing?"

Annie smiled. "I'm making art. But it's going to take a while."

My heart pounded, and I had to lean over to suck in enough air to breathe. My fingers actually itched to reach out and shake her or something. "Then why were you screaming for help?" I sucked in another breath, wondering if I could keep from strangling her. It was so tempting. . . .

"Screaming for help?" She laughed. "No, I was yelling for you to *come* help. It's fun, see?" She motioned to the ground, and I saw an enormous pile of tiny, bright green pieces of new grass. Ladybugs crawled all over the grass, making the piles shift like they were alive.

My pulse still too fast, I stood there panting, staring at what she'd started. The boulder in front of her had some strange markings on it. Trenches and divots that looked sort of like . . . "Dinosaur tracks?" I managed.

"Well, I don't think they're real ones," Annie said, plucking blades of grass a few at a time—ladybugs and all—and placing them in thick beds inside the tracks. "I think they just look that way. But I'm fascinated with the ideas the materials bring— blades of grass and *T. rex* tracks. And living jewels." She held up a ladybug on her finger, but it didn't fly away. "Like, once there was an enormous violent creature that tromped all over everything in its path, and then millions of years later its fossil footprints are filled with freshly picked grass and tiny ladybugs like this one? Don't you like the way it hints at permanent things and ephemeral things at the same time?"

My mind was full. "Ephemeral?"

"Yes," she said, raising one eyebrow. "You know, changing, not lasting . . ."

"I know what it means," I interrupted. And it was true. I knew what it meant. Now, anyway. "What I want to know is why you just ran off like that!" My heart was still racing so hard I could feel it in the back of my throat.

I was close to yelling, really shouting, not caring about the valley or the quiet. If I wasn't careful, I'd be screaming like Laura. This girl was almost making me lose it. "You're so stupid," I said as softly as I could manage. "I thought you were dying!"

"You thought I was dying?" Annie said, standing up so fast flower petals flew all around her. "And here I thought *you* were the stupidest boy in the world. At least you got one thing right."

And she stormed off, leaving me there, staring at her back and down at the ephemeral grass blades in the dinosaur tracks.

That's when it all clicked. Wish girl. *Wish* girl.

Oh, wow. My heart sped back up. All the things she'd said that I hadn't quite understood, all those "wishes" she kept going on about. I hoped I was wrong. But if I was right . . . I had to apologize. I ran after her. It didn't take long to catch up, and when I did, she stopped. She wouldn't look at me, but she was listening. "Annie, I'm sorry," I started.

"Fine," she said. "Whatever. Just go away."

I shook my head, even though she couldn't see. We both began walking back to the flower field. Toward home. After a few minutes, I spoke again. "When you said you were a wish girl, you meant Make-A-Wish, didn't you?"

"Yes," she said. Her voice sounded strange, flat.

My mouth got dry. I knew what Make-A-Wish meant. They only gave those sorts of wishes—for trips to Disney World or the beach or . . . summer camp—to kids who they thought might not get to have the rest of their wishes come true.

Wishes like growing up, going to college, having a family.

Living.

We'd entered the flower field again, and Annie had stopped, soaking in all that color and beauty. I had to ask. "Are you . . . dying?"

She sighed. "I wish," she said, then let out a sad giggle. "Well, not really. Maybe I do. My thing? It's . . . worse, I think. Well, sometimes I think." She sank down in the flowers again.

Worse than dying? I froze, wondering what in the world could be worse. I wasn't going to ask any more questions right then, though. She'd closed her eyes and turned her face up to the sun. I could see darker freckles through the brown of her skin.

My curiosity could wait. I leaned back on my hands and

followed her example, tilting my face up to the sun. It was still fairly cool this low in the valley, and the breeze was much softer. When it moved, though, it carried the scent of thousands of flowers. It smelled like honey and dust. I breathed deeper, letting it fill my lungs.

A few minutes later, Annie spoke, soft as a bee buzzing.

"I have cancer."

I had sort of guessed that.

"I've had it since I was little. It's a kind of leukemia. It started in my bones when I was six. I feel like I've spent most of my life in hospitals. They thought it was in remission. For years. But last month, I started getting headaches."

I nodded, even though she couldn't see me.

"When I went in for my checkup, they found cells in my spinal fluid. Like, a lot. Way more than last time. If they don't do radiation—a lot of radiation soon, and a whole bunch of chemo—they think I might die"

I didn't understand. I knew radiation made people sick or something. But why did she think treating her cancer could be worse than dying? Maybe it was incredibly painful or something. "Does the treatment hurt?" I asked at last.

She breathed out a long, shaky breath. "Well, spinal taps and getting ports put in are no fun, that's for sure. And the days right after chemo . . . " Her face twisted. "But I can handle pain. It's the other part that's scary."

What other part? I wanted to ask. But I didn't. I let the breeze move over me, and I held still. It felt like the whole valley was holding still with me. Waiting.

"It might fix the cancer," she said after a long minute. "It did before. But it's the late effects that have me freaked."

"Late effects?" I'd heard of side effects, sure. But what was this?

"Yeah, stuff that stays with you after. Like a really, really sucky souvenir. 'Welcome to Cancerland, here's your brain damage. Oh, and don't forget to leave all your motor skills when you check out!'"

Brain damage. For real? I remembered my thoughtless comment about how much brain she had left and swallowed hard. Should I apologize again? Or would that make it worse? Like I'd meant it.

"How much?" I asked, watching a bee land on her face and walk around, leaving tiny pollen tracks on her cheek. I didn't try to swat it off; I knew better.

"They don't know," she said, once the bee had gone. "I won't be able to do a lot of things as well, they think." She laughed once. "*Think*. That's one of the things I won't be able to do as well for sure."

I couldn't believe it. This girl who used words I'd never even heard wouldn't be . . . smart anymore? Could it get any worse?

It could.

"I might not be able to walk. I know a girl like that. She has to use a wheelchair now." She shook her head, like she was shaking the thought away. "Like I said, they don't know. Last time, I got off easy. I mean, I have weak joints because of it, so I have to wear those supports." She motioned to her bag, where she'd shoved her ankle wraps earlier. "I used to take dance. I had this stupid dream about being a ballerina. After I got cancer, that was pretty much out of the question."

Annie let out a short, bitter laugh. "Anyway, that's why Mom's letting me run around this weekend and go to camp, even though the doctors really wanted me to start my treatment on Friday. She knows that in a few weeks, I may not be able to run ever again. Or read. Or even draw. Sometimes it affects memory, too. I won't exactly . . . be me anymore. Not like I am now."

She stopped talking, and I could tell she needed to think about something else. I know I did.

I felt it, her need for me to say something, change the subject. And even though my mind was humming louder than the bees, filled with thoughts of things that were worse than dying, I didn't know how to say words that might make her feel better, didn't know if any words existed like that. So I walked to the edge of the clearing and did the only thing I knew how to do well.

I held still and let my stillness be a question.

A wish.

And the valley answered me.

Chapter 10

Something to make her feel better, I'd wished. *Something to distract her.*

A snuffle in the tall flowers, just underneath the shade of the nearest tree, made me hold my breath. An animal was there, rooting around in the shadows, rummaging through the old acorns and dead leaves. "Annie," I whispered as softly as I could when I saw what it was. "Come see."

She heard me, my words carried on the breeze across the meadow. I was glad of her quiet feet; she barely made a sound as she crossed to me. One lifted eyebrow was her only question. I took her hand and led her, silently, into the shadows.

We both dropped to a crouch. She couldn't help it; she let out a happy sigh. I knew how she felt.

The baby armadillo was less than a foot away from our knees. It was no more than six inches long, a soft gray, with tiny black eyes. I was pretty sure it couldn't see us—not well, at least. It hadn't even tried to run away.

"Look at its shell," Annie breathed. She stretched a finger out to touch it but hesitated when the creature sniffed and turned its head. The baby's dimpled shell wasn't hard like an adult armadillo's; I could tell from the wrinkles and folds on the top and sides that it was still pliable. It made me think of the soft spot on Carlie's head when she'd been an infant.

I wasn't worried Annie would hurt it, but I remembered something else. "Don't touch it," I said. "I think armadillos carry leprosy."

Annie smiled and rolled her eyes. "I'm already dying," she said. "I'm not afraid." And she reached out to stroke the armadillo.

It didn't run away, just kept shuffling around at our feet for twenty minutes like it had forgotten what it was supposed to be doing. By then Annie had taken out her sketchbook and done a quick picture of it, of course.

"It's exquisite," she said, standing up, wiping the leaf mulch off her knees.

"Yes," I said. I knew what she meant. Armadillos weren't exactly beautiful, but this one, so small . . .

"I didn't even ask if you wanted to draw it." Annie pushed her sketchbook toward me. "Do you draw?"

"No, I stink at art."

"Well, what are you good at? Playing music?"

I wanted to laugh. I shook my head.

"I know," Annie said suddenly. "You write."

I couldn't help it, I shivered. "Not anymore."

"Why not?" Annie put her sketchpad away, but she was watching my face, waiting. "What happened?"

"Nothing," I lied, remembering the last thing I'd written. The thing that had made my mom and dad go nuts, that had turned my life upside down.

All of our lives.

Time to change the subject again. I pointed to the armadillo. "Do you think its mother is looking for it?" I peered into the darker shadows of the trees nearer the stream. A shadow, small and low to the ground, moved restlessly there. "She is," I answered my own question. "We'd better let it go back." I took Annie's hand again, and we both stepped away, watching as the baby disappeared in the shade.

"Thank you," I whispered to the valley, soft enough that Annie wouldn't hear. I didn't want her thinking I was as crazy as the Colonel's wife.

Although I was starting to wonder myself.

We walked slowly across the meadow. There was some sort of path I'd missed before, in between the trees ahead, with great looping grapevines hanging from them. I could see clusters of unripe grapes decorating the vines. Annie seemed to know everything, so I asked her when they would be ripe. "I don't know," she answered, running one hand along a vine as thick as her wrist, testing it to see if it would hold her weight. It did.

She found a loop low enough to sit on and sat down, using the vine as a swing. "Push me."

I had to laugh. She'd sounded just like Carlie when she would yell, "Peep!" and hold out her arms for me to pick her up. Maybe girls learned how to do that princess voice when they were a month old or something. "Your wish is my command."

Annie smiled and said, "That's right, all my wishes must come true. And if you push me long enough, maybe I'll make one of yours come true, too. But don't count on it, serf."

I pushed her for a while, high enough that the grapevines protested and slipped a little. "So, Peter Stone," she said, hopping off. "If you could make one wish, what would you wish for?"

I answered without thinking. It was the one thing I'd been wishing for years. Especially since I'd discovered the valley, since I had felt what real quiet was like. "I wish I could just be alone. Like, feel the peace and quiet. For a long time. Not have to share it with anyone. Not have to worry about anyone ruining it." Not ever have to go home, I didn't say. Of course, I was thinking about my family, how they wouldn't get it—wouldn't understand the beauty in the quiet. Never would, I figured.

But Annie didn't know that.

As soon as the words were out of my mouth and I saw her face, I realized what I'd said. "Wait," I tried, "I didn't mean *you*. I meant other people. My sister, and—hey, don't leave!" Too late.

"Your wish is my command," she threw back over her shoulder as she hurried away. "I won't bother you anymore, Stone Boy." I could hear tears in her voice. I kicked the ground, and a bee zipped up out of nowhere and stung me on the hand.

"Ouch!" I yelled, pulling the stinger out and squeezing the sting. "I'm sorry," I called again, just short of a yell. "You don't have to leave!"

She was already gone. By the time I'd crossed the meadow, gotten stung by another bee, and started back up the hill, I knew there was no hope.

I couldn't catch her, and no matter how fast I ran, I couldn't outpace the cloud of angry gnats that followed me.

Their sharp bites made me feel on the outside just like I felt inside. All chewed up.

I was such a jerk. The valley seemed to think so, too. I tripped twenty times on the way back, rocks that seemed perfectly stable slipping at the last second. My knees and hands were scraped bloody by the time I got to the top.

Of course, then I realized I'd climbed the wrong hill. My house wasn't over the rise on this one. Instead, there was another house smack dab in front of me, a strange triangular-shaped one, painted red with white trim.

And this one also had an old woman standing at the front door, holding a shotgun. Pointing it at me.

Chapter 11

"This is private property, boy," the woman said, soft but clear. I didn't look at her face; I was too concerned with the gun. "*My* property."

"Sorry, ma'am," I managed, though how I didn't know. My mouth was drier than cotton. "I think I'm lost."

"You've been down in the valley, haven't you?" She laughed. "The valley threw you out. You're pretty beat up. That'll teach you to trespass on my land. You're lucky it didn't pierce your ears—or something else—with porcupine quills." *Uh-oh. This must be the Colonel's wife*, I thought. The crazy one.

She looked crazy enough, dressed in a pair of old overalls and a long-sleeved shirt, with her black-and-gray hair stuck in a bun on the top of her head and held by what appeared to be a dirty stick. She walked closer, feet clomping in big, mud-stained brown men's boots, and lowered the gun. "I thought you were one of them boys that's been killing birds over there. But you're new. Where do you live?"

"Um." I looked around. "On one of the hills?" I managed. I didn't even know my address. "There's this fence made out of railroad ties."

"Oh, the old Carlson place! I wondered who'd been suckered into renting that pile of junk lumber."

"My mom and dad," I said. "Maxine and Joshua Stone." I paused, wondering if I could ask her to put the gun away.

"Do you hunt, boy?"

Why was she asking this? Then I thought about the gunshots Annie and I had heard. Maybe it had been the Colonel's wife shooting, after all. Maybe she'd been out hunting . . . but for what? "No," I answered.

"Own a gun?"

"No," I repeated, backing away slowly. "I've never actually shot one." And I didn't want to see a demonstration either.

She wasn't letting me get away that easy, and she matched my backward steps with slow, steady paces toward me. "Ever shot a bird before in your life? Or killed one? Ever drowned a kitten or dropped a puppy in a creek?"

"No," I said, my stomach twisting. She *was* crazy. "That's horrible! Why are you asking me this?"

She clicked something—not the trigger, thank goodness; the safety?—and slung the gun over one shoulder. "Well, you're all bit up from my valley. You did something to earn those bee stings."

Oh. "I said something to Annie I shouldn't have."

"The little cancer girl?" The Colonel's wife gave me a beady glare. "You like being mean to sick girls, is that it?"

"No!" I sputtered. "No, I don't. I was trying to tell her what I loved about the valley, how it was magi—how it was special," I substituted. *Magic* sounded crazy. But from the gleam in her eye, the Colonel's wife knew what I'd been about to say. "I was trying to tell her why I liked going in the valley . . . and she took it wrong. I need to find her and apologize."

"Well, any kid who can see the valley's . . . *specialness* can't be all bad, bee stings or no," she said at last. She clomped away toward the house and motioned for me to follow. "Kid, you're a good ways from home. And it's almost as far to that camp Annie's going to. Get in my go-kart, and I'll take you home. You can chase after the girl tomorrow. If I know girls—and I do, having been one back in the Stone Age—she won't listen to any of your stories until at least Tuesday. Give her time to cool off."

The Colonel's wife was going to take me home. I felt simultaneously relieved and terrified.

I knew I shouldn't get in a car with a stranger. And this woman was certainly strange. But it wasn't a car, as I saw a few minutes later. It was the most amazing monster go-kart I'd ever seen. And it was getting late. My parents were going to kill me, and I had no idea at all how to find my house. I had to trust someone.

She handed me a helmet to match hers—both of them painted black with red and orange flames—and told me to "strap in." I buckled up and hung on to the foam-wrapped side bar where the door should have been attached.

I held on for my life. Whether she was really crazy or not, the woman drove like a maniac for sure. Over the wind and the roar of the engine—it sounded like forty leaf blowers all working at the same time—I heard her yell, "Yee-haw!" just in time to take an enormous downhill. My stomach dropped to my feet— it was as scary and fast as any roller coaster I'd ever been on.

A corner was coming up, a sharp one. We were going way too fast. For a second, I wondered if she was trying to kill me, if we were going to crash. But she slammed on the brakes at the last second, fishtailing just a little bit on some gravel near the edge of the road, and then gunned it again on the next uphill.

After a few minutes, I forgot to be scared. This was the most fun I'd had since . . . well, possibly ever.

"There's cancer girl's camp," I heard over the rush of the wind. The Colonel's wife was pointing across a smaller valley at a red-painted barn surrounded by a few goat-shed-looking things. Were those the cabins? There was a muddy-edged lake— more like a pond—with a fishing boat tied to a stake at one end.

Definitely not a swimming hole. And there weren't any horses or gardens or . . . anything, from what I could see.

It wasn't what I had expected for a Make-A-Wish camp. In fact, it sort of . . . stunk. That was the best they could do for a bunch of kids dying of cancer?

"Your house is just over there," the Colonel's wife shouted. She pulled up to the top of the hill and cut the engine. "See it?"

It was there, the roof barely visible over the oak trees in front of it. "Yes, I see it," I said, wondering why she'd stopped.

"Well, get out and get going then," she said. "I've got a beef with some other boys that live two more hills over. Bird killers. Heard them shooting earlier. If I hurry, I can catch them before they get back home." She grinned and reached behind her, placing her shotgun on the seat I vacated.

I barely had a second to pitch my helmet into the cart before she peeled out, kicking up little bits of gravel and a cloud of exhaust and dust.

After she had gone, and the motor's roar had faded into the distance, I realized just how quiet the valley had been. On this side of the hill, I could hear lots of manmade sounds: a lawn mower, music playing from a radio station . . . my mom calling my name with a side of panic and a whole helping of mad-as-heck.

Uh-oh. I ran for the house, wishing once more that I was in the valley, surrounded by wind, birds, the rustling of leaves, and Annie's laughter.

Chapter 12

I was grounded for the rest of my life, Mom said. She sent me to my room for the evening. But then loudmouth Laura reminded Mom that was where I liked to be most, so she changed her mind, making me stay in the living room with the family.

The living room was the noisiest part of the house. Carlie had a set of wooden blocks she was using to clack together while Dad watched *Die Hard* at full volume. Mom was slamming around drawers on her filing cabinets in the corner of the room she'd decided to use for an office, and Laura had staked out the phone. How she could even hear what her friend was saying with all the noise was beyond me.

I had a headache, of course. And that reminded me of Annie. Her headaches must have been much worse. And I had made her feel awful. How could I apologize? Even though I knew where the camp was now, I couldn't get there since Mom would be watching me like a hawk.

I didn't understand why she cared about me being gone. I hadn't gotten hurt. And it wasn't like she had told me she'd planned some big family brunch in Austin. If I'd known she'd made plans that included me, I wouldn't have run off.

Probably.

I sighed and rubbed at the headache acupressure spot again. Even if I could get to Annie, I wasn't sure how to tell her I was sorry. She had looked so upset. Crying, I thought. I had made a Make-A-Wish girl cry. It didn't get much more awful than that.

I sort of deserved the headache.

The next day, I got more than I deserved: Carlie Stone, cutting two teeth, for nine hours while Mom went to work.

"Laura," I repeated at the bathroom door. "Would you please come out? I have to get a spare diaper for Carlie." My repeated attempts to dislodge Laura from the bathroom all morning so that I could use it had gone unanswered. I'd ended up using a bush outside, much to Carlie's delight. Of course, the possibility of outdoor peeing had made her so excited that she'd refused to wear a diaper since. Now she'd started shredding them the second I put them on her.

"I said just a minute," Laura yelled.

"It's been an hour and a half!" I surprised myself by raising my voice. Surprised my dad, too, it turned out.

"Wow, was that you, Peter?" He fake-punched me on the arm as he walked down the hall, carrying an old amplifier he'd bought for Laura at a garage sale a few months before, so she could play while he drummed. "Try not to burst my eardrums."

I glared at his back. That amp was one of the reasons we'd been evicted, I thought. I should have cut through the cord when Dad first brought it home. It would have saved me a lot of trouble.

"Peep!" Carlie had escaped from her playpen—her new trick for the day—and was standing at my side, buck naked.

"Carlie, really? Five diapers? I'm just gonna use a pillowcase."

I had a thought: *Laura's pillowcase would do.*

I had worked it halfway off her pillow when I heard Dad call out my name. "Peter? You've got company."

Company? Annie! I dropped the pillow, wrapped the pillowcase around Carlie and tucked her under one arm, then ran to the front of the house. The front door was wide open, and Dad was right outside, talking to someone.

It wasn't Annie, though. I could hear male voices. Boys?

"Here ya go, Carlie," I whispered, plunking her down in the playpen and handing her a few graham crackers. She wasn't supposed to eat them outside of the high chair—Mom said they turned into cookie cement when she chewed them up—but I didn't have a diaper for her, and I wasn't going to meet strangers at the door holding a naked baby.

When I got to the door, I was even more glad I'd left Carlie behind.

Because the two kids right outside were holding a dead turkey vulture. They were the bird killers.

❧

I didn't know what to think—besides *gross*. The kid holding the dead bird by its feet was taller than me, tall enough that the head of the bird just brushed the dirt as he held it. He looked older, too, maybe fourteen. The other kid was ten, maybe eleven, but he had a hard glint in his eye that I'd seen in some kids in San Antonio. Like he might want to punch me in the stomach to see what I'd had for breakfast. Definitely not a normal ten-year-old.

The guys looked me over, and I saw the older kid try to hide a smile. That was when I realized I was still holding Carlie's most recent torn-up diaper. I tossed it back through the doorway and stepped out into the sunshine.

"Hey, Peter," Dad said, oblivious to the looks the guys were giving me—and him. "These two boys live just down the road a mile or so. I met their parents at the gas station when your mom and I checked the place out the first time. Remember I told you about them? Why don't you go play with them for a while?"

The younger kid laughed once and repeated, "Yeah, come *play* with us."

"I'm grounded," I reminded Dad in an undertone. I didn't even mention the giant dead bird the older kid was swinging back and forth, its reddish-pink head smearing the dust with blood.

"Well, you're ungrounded now," Dad said, reaching behind my back to shove me out the door. I tripped over the stoop and almost fell forward onto one of the kids. "They invited you over to their house. What your mother doesn't know won't hurt her. Just be back by lunch."

He shut the door before I could even come up with an excuse other than "These boys look like trouble," which was what I was thinking.

"So, you're Peter," the younger one said. "I'm Jake."

"I'm Doug," the other one said, swinging the vulture a little harder now, toward me. The head of the poor thing brushed my knee. I could tell Doug was waiting to see what I would do. If I would freak out. I just shrugged and stepped to the side so the vulture wouldn't crack me in the stomach on the next swing.

"You like to hunt?" Jake asked, stepping with me. I started walking down the driveway, but not too fast. Jake pulled something out of his pocket—a Twizzler—and stuck it in his mouth so it hung out like a cigarette.

"I don't have a gun," I said. "Do you?"

"How'd you think we killed this buzzard?" Doug asked. He talked slowly, like he had to think over each word before it came out. "With our hands?" Then they both laughed.

"Let's try that next time," Jake said. He looked at me, waiting for me to speak.

"I'd like to see that," I lied. I couldn't imagine looking at a bird and thinking, *I'd like to kill that.* Birds just seemed . . . too fragile, and beautiful. Not that I would ever tell these boys, or anyone, I felt that way.

"What kind of guns you got?" I said instead.

"Pellet rifles," Jake said. "Dad took our .22 away after the cat." He darted that glance at me again, the one that dared me to say something.

The cat? I wasn't even going to ask. We kept walking, down the road and toward a street where I thought I'd seen some sort of mobile home. "So, you're supposed to be grounded," Jake said, kicking at a rock. "Your parents just what? Take away your TV and stuff?"

"Yeah," I said. "And I get all the chores."

"Just grounded, huh? Nothing worse?"

"Um, no."

"Must be nice," he mumbled and wiped his nose on his arm. "Wish my dad would stop with just grounding me."

Getting grounded was *nice?* I wondered what happened to these guys when they got in trouble. I was going to say something, but Jake glanced up at me with a cold gleam in his eye that froze my tongue.

"What'd you get grounded for?" Doug asked. He hefted the vulture over one shoulder.

I swallowed. "I ran off."

"Where to?" Doug asked, chewing on the Twizzler. He kept rubbing the end in his hands, twisting it around his nails and fingertips. His hands were covered with dirt and blood. From the vulture, I assumed.

"There's this valley," I started, "with no houses—"

"The valley of death?" Doug hooted. "No way!"

The valley of death? I shook my head, wondering if they meant some other place. My valley was anything but. "I don't think so. It was just a big valley with a stream at the bottom, some kind of big trees, and—"

"That's it!" Jake said. "Whoa, you got all the way to the bottom of the valley of death?" He examined me, cataloguing all the mosquito bites, scratches, and bee stings. Come to think of it, both the boys were covered with bites and stings, like they'd been attacked.

"Looks like you got stung up pretty bad down there, didn't ya?" Jake said. "Us too. Be careful. Bugs are the least of it. That valley's got the best hunting, but . . . " His eyes cut to his brother. "Bad things happen to ya if you go down in it. Things that don't make sense."

"I got that feeling," I said. Then I remembered the gunshots from the day before. "Have you gone hunting over there?"

"Yesterday," Doug said. "Rabbit. Almost got it. Until the bugs."

The bugs? I almost asked, but then I realized: When the mosquitoes and wasps had flown up the hill, like they were late for something . . . they were going to sting these kids. To chase them out of the valley.

So the valley *was* magic. It knew things.

I didn't say anything as we walked, but Jake kept talking, like I'd asked a question. "We found the rabbit on this side of the hill, but then it ran into the valley—they know they're safe over there."

"Think it," Doug said.

"Yeah, for now they're safe. But we figured something out with the buzzard here," and Jake took one of the vulture's wings and stretched it out. "We climbed just to the top of the hill for this one. It was sitting on a dead branch barely down in the valley. We were so close—"

"So close!" Doug giggled.

"Shut up, I'm telling it. We were right over him. The wind was coming from the valley like it does. Didn't smell us. We weren't quite in the valley, see? So it couldn't get after us. And we went right up behind this vulture with our pellet rifles."

"Bam!" Doug said, shaking the bird.

"What are you going to do with it?" I nodded toward the bird, wishing I didn't feel so much like throwing up every time I looked down at it. It wasn't a beautiful creature up close. It was scraggly, its head reminding me of an angry old man's. But I'd seen thousands of turkey vultures flying overhead, soaring on heat currents. To kill one just for fun . . . it was sick.

"Well, we ain't gonna eat it," Doug said. "Turkey buzzard'll make ya sick." He said it like he knew.

Jake nodded. "We're gonna go throw it up on Old Lady Empson's porch. The Colonel's wife."

They were going to dump a dead bird on a harmless—okay, slightly crazy—old woman's doorstep? "Why?"

"Hate her," Doug said as Jake peered off into the distance at something. "She got my gun taken."

"Taken?"

"Told Dad I was shooting pets."

"Oh," I said, remembering his comment. "Did you shoot her cat or something?"

Doug didn't answer, just laughed, and swung the dead bird around his head like he was going to throw it at me. I ducked.

I was going to be sick if I hung around these guys for a second longer.

"Hey, I got a better idea," Jake said. "Let's take it to the summer camp. We can throw it in the pool. They'll hate it."

"The Make-A-Wish camp?" I wasn't sure I could get any more horrified. Who had raised these kids, Jack the Ripper and Freddy Krueger?

"Nah, it's Doublecreek," Jake said, reaching for the final tip of Doug's Twizzler. Considering, he held it out to me. "Want the last bite?"

I think he was trying to be nice. I shook my head and muttered, "No, thanks."

"Isn't the camp for kids with cancer, though?" I said after

he'd given the last bit back to Doug, who stuck it in his mouth with the same hand he'd been using to hold the dead vulture. Then he licked his finger.

"Nah, it's just an arts-and-crafts camp. Why'd you think it was cancer kids?"

"I met someone," I started, then trailed off. I didn't want to tell these guys about Annie.

"Who?" Jake said. His eyes had gotten sharp again. "A girl?"

"I—I gotta go," I said instead and held my hands to my middle.

"What's wrong?" Doug asked as he slung the dead vulture over one shoulder.

Where should I start? I wondered. "I think I'm sick," I said. "Bad. Diarrhea. I got to get home."

"Just go in the bushes, Peter," Jake yelled at my back as I hurried away. I could hear him and his brother laughing and making fun of me almost all the way home—sound travels in the country. But I didn't care as long as it took their mind off the camp. I had to warn Annie to stay away from these guys. I had to apologize, too.

But I was grounded for forever, and I didn't know when I'd have another shot like this morning. Dad didn't expect me until lunchtime.

I could cut cross-country, get to the camp . . . and find out why the two guys who lived here full-time didn't think it was a Make-A-Wish camp.

Had Annie lied to me? She was practically a stranger, after all. Maybe she was the crazy one, not the Colonel's wife.

But as I slipped under a strand of barbed wire and ran behind a line of trees toward the camp, I knew the craziest ones on this side of the hill were the ones I'd just left, carrying a dead vulture around with them.

Crazy. And maybe dangerous, too.

Chapter 13

I could hear the music before I could see the camp buildings through the trees. It was . . . lousy. Like somebody had learned to play the guitar in three easy lessons and thought that qualified them to inflict it on others. Sort of like my sister's playing a few months back.

I stopped sneaking and started walking more confidently as the buildings came into view; I didn't want anyone seeing me to think I was lurking or anything. On closer inspection, the goat sheds weren't sheds at all. Just cabins with metal roofs that needed a new coat of paint or three.

The barn was where the music was coming from. It must have been where the campers were. I walked slowly to the big double doors, open to let the breeze in, and stood just to one side so my eyes could adjust to the darker room.

There were long tables set up inside, covered with craft supplies—every size of popsicle stick and color of yarn imaginable, construction paper and newsprint in stacks, as well as a row of hot-glue guns, felt, and fabric scraps. The place looked like it could keep a kindergarten class in art supplies until the apocalypse.

But the kids sitting at the tables were all older. Too old for popsicle-stick crafts. Third grade and up, I figured, from their sizes. And all girls.

Ack. I hadn't figured on this being an all-girls camp. I guess it made sense.

"May I help you?" The counselor—or at least the oldest person in the room—stood up and walked toward me. She looked strong—like she'd gone to college on a volleyball scholarship or something—but friendly. "Are you lost?"

"No, ma'am," I answered. The girls at the table had all started laughing. Except Annie—she sat at the end of the table, sort of removed from the others. She was making something—the same thing the other kids were, I saw, except hers was finished. It was some sort of yarn thing, done on sticks. She didn't look at me. Wouldn't.

"Can I help you?" the counselor repeated, stern now.

"Oh, n-n-no," I stammered, then took a deep breath. "It's just . . . I heard my cousin was in camp here this week. I wanted to say hi. I live near here."

"Your cousin?" She turned. "Is this someone's cousin?"

"I'll be his cousin!" one of the girls shouted. The other girls all yelled, "Oooooo!" and I could feel myself blushing.

Annie stood up. "I'm his cousin." Suddenly, the table fell silent. The other girls stopped joking, wouldn't even look at her. What had Annie done to make everyone hate her in just a few hours?

Then I thought about her bossiness, her illness, and her bright, curly red hair and realized she probably didn't have to *do* much at all. "Can she come outside and talk?" I asked the counselor. "I can't stay long anyway."

"Well . . . he's your cousin? Living all the way out here?" The counselor shook her head. "I guess for a few minutes. You've already finished your major art project for the day, huh?" She took Annie's yarn thing, looked at it, and handed it back to her. "You're quite the little artist, Annie Blythe. That's the best God's-eye I've seen in years."

"Thanks," Annie said, shouldering past. She didn't wait for me, just walked through the barn doors. I followed. Annie headed for the murky lake.

If she's going to kill me and throw the body in, I guess that would be the best place to hide it, I thought, snorting.

"What?" She stopped and sneaked a look at me.

I told her what I'd been thinking, and she laughed, too. "I won't kill you. Even though you might deserve it."

We sat on the edge of a shaky wooden platform that was mired in the mud at one end of the lake and watched the dragonflies and wasps buzz over the top of the water and duckweed for a while.

Then Annie spoke. "Why did you come here?"

"To rescue you from yarn art," I said at last. "And to say I'm sorry. I didn't mean what I said."

Annie held up a hand. "It's okay. I thought about it, and I get what you meant. It's the same reason I went to the valley anyway." She smiled a little, staring at the lake. "The first time I saw you there, at Serendipity Pool, I was so mad. I thought I was the first person in the world to find that spot."

"Serendipity Pool?"

"Yeah," she said, taking the end of the yarn on her project and unwinding it slowly. She grabbed a flower and tied it to the loose end of the yarn, then lowered it toward the water, unrolling yarn like it was fishing line. "What do you think? Serendipity Pool? Or maybe Effervescent Springs?"

"Why name it?"

Annie shrugged. "I don't know, it makes it more real. Anyway, I've been reading through my list of favorite words, and those are some of the top ones."

"Your list of favorite words?" I smiled. Trust Annie to have something like that.

"Yes." She twitched the yarn so the flower on the end made small ripples. "I've always loved difficult words, especia—"

"I figured that much," I interrupted. "I can't tell what you're saying half the time."

"If you please?" She waited to see if I was finished, like a teacher. I stuck my tongue out at her.

"Fine. I've always loved words, especially beautiful ones. Mellifluous words. Actually, *mellifluous* is one of my favorites."

"What does it mean?"

"Sweet-sounding. Try it—say it. Doesn't it actually sound sweet on your tongue, like a piece of taffy or something?" We sat there, saying the word *mellifluous* under our breaths for a few seconds. I felt sort of stupid doing it, but no one else was around. And she was right. It almost tasted sweet.

"Try *sumptuous*," Annie said, "or *susurrus*. Or my new favorite, since I came to camp: *lachrymose*."

"Lachrymose?" I knew that one—it had been on a spelling test the year before. It meant something that caused tears. "Are the other campers being mean?"

"Yes. Well, no," Annie said softly. "Not really. I'm just not exactly a people person these days. They think I'm weird, of course. I have to rest a lot, and the counselors told the other kids about my leukemia. My mom made a scene this morning. She has separation issues."

"That stinks." I asked the question I'd been wondering. "So, this isn't really Make-A-Wish camp, right?"

"No," Annie said. "It's not. You only get one real wish. I got my wish granted when I was eight after I went into remission— that trip to New York I told you about. It was supposed to be this big celebration. Yahoo, I survived. So I went to every museum I could find. I saw a lot of amazing art up there. Real art."

"They won't give you another trip—another wish? Not even . . . now?" That didn't seem fair.

"Nah," Annie said, standing up and reeling the yarn back in slowly. "One wish per customer. Mom's bankrolling this one. Which was nice, I guess. I only wish . . . "

"What?"

"Well, this was supposed to be art camp." She laughed. "To be honest, we didn't have a lot of time to research it. The doctors were mad my mom let me come at all. We thought I'd be painting, sculpting . . . "

"You won't be doing that stuff later in the week?" I had been hoping for her sake it was going to build up to something cool.

"Sure, sculpting with Play-Doh." Annie sighed. "I want to go back to the valley." She arched one eyebrow. "Want to run away with me? I've got a sleeping bag and a canteen. All I need are some granola bars and I'm fine for at least a week."

"A week? We'd need more than granola bars and a sleeping bag." I thought back to a list I'd made the year before. It had been pretty long. "We'd also have to have a backpack, a knife maybe, some water purification tablets—"

"A fishing hook?"

"You going to gut your own fish?" I asked. "I'm not gonna gut yours *and* mine."

Annie made a face. "Ew. No. So we're back to granola bars then. Or staying here." As she glared at the cabins behind us, I saw something in her eyes—hopelessness? I'd felt that way before. Trapped.

Back then I'd tried to find a way out. But when I'd finally started writing my plan of how to get away, even if I hadn't meant to go through with it . . . it had all gone wrong. Now I was every bit as trapped as Annie. At least I didn't have to do string art.

"Looks like we're stuck here," I said, pushing her slightly toward the water. "Let me know when you're willing to gut a fish, and I'll help you make a break for it."

"Promise?"

It was weird. I knew we were only kidding, but she sounded like she meant it. She must really hate camp. "Sure," I said. "Just say the word."

"What word? *Lachrymose?*"

"No. Fish guts."

She laughed and didn't even tease me about it being two words. A small perch was nibbling at her flower, but she pulled it up before it could bite. "So no running away . . . yet," she said. "But, Peter, I've been thinking. I want to go back to the valley and make some real art. I could turn that whole place into an exhibit—sketch it and even photograph it. I brought a camera." Annie paused. "We could do it together."

I didn't know what to say. I didn't really want to spend my whole summer hanging out with her, but I did sort of owe her an apology . . . and making *real* art, whatever that was, sounded fun.

"Can you sneak out?" I asked softly. I had seen the counselor come out of the barn. She was searching for us.

Annie got a look of wicked determination. "I will. Tomorrow, or maybe the day after. Wait for me at . . . Evanescent Pond?"

"Nah," I said. "Serendipity Pool sounds better."

"Everybody's a critic," Annie shot back. Then "Coming!" she yelled to the counselor, who was calling in earnest now. She turned to me. "Swimming is in the afternoons, and I'll 'fail' the swim test today. I'll play the poor-little-sick-girl routine, get them to let me nap instead."

"Nap?"

She shrugged. "I have my own cabin, at least. Mom insisted. Nobody will know if I'm gone. I'll tell them my headache meds make me sleep for hours. Look for me around two, okay?"

I wasn't going to tell her I was grounded. If she was going to have to trick an entire camp full of people to sneak out, I could figure out how to get around my dad.

"I'll be there," I said. "But I'm still not certain what you mean about making the valley into art. It's already pretty."

"Art isn't pretty," Annie said, whirling around. "It's transformative! Real art changes you—whether you like it or not. Real art isn't"—she looked down at the yarn thing in her hand—"it's not just wrapping yarn around sticks, or coloring in the lines. Real art makes a difference. It has meaning. I'll show you tomorrow."

"Are you done here, Annie?" The counselor had reached us.

She was trying not to look alarmed at Annie's passionate out-burst, but she wasn't doing a very good job. "It's time to make our seashell picture frames. You won't want to miss that."

Annie gave me a despairing glance. I knew the feeling. It was the way I imagined I looked every time Laura and Dad cranked up the amps, every time Mom and Dad started fighting. A headache was definitely coming.

"You live close enough to walk?" The counselor's voice was suspicious. "Where, exactly?"

I made a vague motion toward Doug and Jake's house. "About a half mile that way."

The counselor shook her head. "What do you do out here all day?"

I thought about the valley, and being still, and knew this woman would never understand it. "I hunt," I lied, trying to think of what Jake would say. My heart started beating fast as I spoke. I had to cover the shakiness in my voice, so I made my Texas accent thick enough to slice. "Mostly varmints. Armadillos. Buzzards. That sort of thing. With my pellet rifle."

The counselor looked repulsed. "Really?"

"Yup," I said, hiking up my shorts with my thumbs. Was I overdoing it? Annie's eyes were bulging out. Was she mad? Maybe I should run off now, before I was busted . . .

The counselor's eyes were bulging, too. "What do you . . . do with them?"

I had to keep going, so I shrugged. "Possum's good eatin'. You want me to bring you some?"

"No!"

I could hear Annie stifle a laugh. "Bye, cousin," I said to Annie, who was being dragged away by the counselor.

"Tell Aunt Mabel and Uncle Fester hi for me, Cousin Petey," Annie yelled over her shoulder, the twinkle back in her eye. "And don't forget to invite me over for possum stew next weekend."

"I won't," I called back.

I ran home, wondering at how good I felt. Two days before, I'd been annoyed at the thought of Annie hanging around in the valley. My valley. And now? The thought of her being there stretched a grin across my whole face.

I spent that night on a dictionary-and-thesaurus site looking up big, beautiful words and staring at pictures of outdoor art installations until Laura kicked me off the computer.

I thought I understood what Annie was talking about.

"How did you like hanging out with those boys?" Dad whispered after dinner, once Mom was out of the room. I got it: He hadn't told her he'd ungrounded me. "What were their names?"

"Doug and Jake," I said. "You know, they shot that vulture."

"Yeah, cool, huh?" He looked a little uncertain, but happy.

Cool was not the word I would have used. *Cruel*, maybe. "Um, okay."

"Well, they seemed nice enough, a little rough-and-tumble."

Dad ran a hand over the top of his head like he was checking the size of his bald spot. "But I think it would be good for you to have some guy friends. Maybe you could invite them over here tomorrow."

Invite them over? They'd probably torture Carlie for fun. I was never, ever going to invite them into the house.

Dad was waiting for me to say something. I just shrugged. He cleared his throat. "You know, I worry sometimes that you didn't have many friends in San Antonio. That was probably at the root of all the . . . problems. This might be a good chance to start over. These guys could end up being your best friends."

Best friends? I wanted to puke. Should I tell him about the cat and what they'd planned to do with the vulture? Should I say what I really thought? It would probably just disappoint him again. He didn't get me; he never had.

For all I knew, he wanted me to be just like those kids. He'd probably offer to buy me a gun next.

"I was thinking," Dad said, walking across to the doorway and peering through it, like he was checking for eavesdroppers. "I know it's been hard to move here. You don't have anybody to hang out with."

I never hung out with anyone to begin with, I wanted to say. I didn't speak, but the same thought was there, in Dad's eyes. He couldn't understand; Dad was one of those guys everyone liked, always laughing and yelling, staying out with his musician friends whenever he and Mom could get Laura to babysit.

Me? I hadn't even had friends in elementary school, except for a couple of girls who moved away in second grade. Nobody liked the quiet kid, the serious one. I had been that way since I was born, as far as I could figure. I'd seen my baby pictures; I wasn't smiling in almost any of them.

The silence stretched uncomfortably long until Dad cleared his throat. "I had an idea. A way you could make friends, maybe with those two guys. How would you like me to get you a pellet rifle?"

I almost laughed. He was so predictable. "Maybe later, Dad," I said. I had an idea, but my palms started to sweat just considering it.

I was going to lie to Dad. I had never lied to him, not really. I took a quick breath. "Um, actually, the guys have an extra one. They invited me to come hunting with them tomorrow afternoon. I told them I was grounded. . . . "

"Can you be back in by five?" Dad whispered. I nodded, hoping he didn't notice my red face.

"Then you go." Dad smiled. "I always wanted to hunt when I was a kid. Never got to. What are you going to shoot?"

I remembered Annie's comment: It was nothing-at-all season. "Um, varmints," I said. "Pests. Rats, maybe." Did they even have rats out here? I hoped Dad wouldn't ask any more questions about hunting. I didn't even know how to shoot a real gun; I sure didn't want him volunteering to come with us and show me. "Maybe a rabbit."

"Awesome," he said, then gave me a weird side hug. "My son, the hunter."

Huh. Finally, I was doing something Dad approved of. Or at least he thought I was.

What a jerk.

But, hey! At least I was going to be able to return to the valley. And even though I was sneaking off to do it, I had a feeling making art with Annie would give me the chance to do something I never thought I could do, without running away.

I could be happy.

Chapter 14

Sneaking off the next day was the easy part. Making art? With no paint, no paper, no supplies of any kind? Way harder.

When I got to the pool that afternoon, Annie wasn't there. I thought I would try to figure out what we could use to make art in the wild, but there wasn't anything. Just water, rocks, leaves, and an enormous bullfrog that made as much noise as Carlie on a bad day. I plucked a few strands of grass and wove them into a small ring, then made more as I waited, setting the wreaths to float on the surface of the water. It didn't take long for little minnows to start nibbling at them and then to begin jumping through the rings, like miniature dolphins at SeaWorld.

I smiled. The leaping minnows glittered in the patchy sunlight, splashing more than I thought they could, making an un-fishlike amount of sound. *Pretty loud*, I thought. *I'm impressed.*

After a moment, birds started singing like it was a contest or something, and the insects in the bushes buzzed and hummed so much, it almost made my teeth shake. I'd never thought of nature as noisy. I moved down, closer to the pool, and realized something. The stone lip that jutted out on the side of the water was making all the sounds louder. Maybe we should call it Amplification Pool. Or Reverberation Pond. Or—

"Hey, Stone Boy!" Annie had arrived at last. "Whatcha doin'?"

"Nothing."

"Well, we have about two hours before the camp counselors start freaking out about where I'm at, so let's get down into the valley and start making art." She leaned down, ripped her ankle supports off, and stuffed them in her bag. The tone of her voice made me look at her face more closely. Her features were drawn tight, like she had to hold her lips and eyes close together to keep something from escaping. Anger, or pain.

"What happened, Annie?" I stood up and jumped across the rocks to her side. "Bad day?"

"You could say that," she said. "But art makes everything better. I learned that in New York."

She started down into the valley, and I followed. I didn't ask for details; I hated it when people pressed me to tell them more than I was ready. She'd get to it. Or not. It was her story to tell. Sure enough, by the time we'd gotten to the stream at the base of the hill, Annie started talking.

"So, when I was six, I got sick. They thought it was pretty bad." She laughed once. "Little did they know . . . Anyway, treatment takes about two years, two and a half, until they'll use words like *remission*. I had been pestering Mom to take me to the modern art museum in Houston, and when I went there, I just . . . fell in love with art. So Mom got in touch with Make-A-Wish, and they sent me up to New York to visit the big ones. It was amazing. I never knew you could make things that moved people, out of anything. Canvas, sure, but they also made art out of trash, and concrete and graffiti, and natural stuff—stones, sticks, leaves. . . . " She stopped. "Hey, mud!"

We'd reached the edge of the stream bank, and Annie pressed her hands down into the silty soil that spread like a mud beach on one side of the gently flowing water. "This could totally work as glue later this week. But what to use for today's project . . . " She was off again, darting back and forth, looking for something. Then she found it. "Fossils!" The streambed was littered with limestone fossils—clamshell-shaped ones, snails, and stones with little embedded ammonites. "Okay, Stone Boy, this is your job." All the pain was gone from her voice now. Annie was on a mission. I sighed. I had a feeling her mission was going to be hard work for me.

"We'll need as many of these fossils as you can find. At least a hundred," she said, confirming my suspicion.

"What for?"

"We're going to make fossil cairns," she said and ran off, like I had any idea what she meant. What was a cairn, anyway?

I took off my shoes and set them by the stream, then waded

in, looking for fossils. When I'd found a couple, I'd tuck them into my pockets. But that only worked for so long. Soon, I had a sizeable pile on the bank. It was weird: At first glance, it hadn't seemed like there were that many fossils to find. But after a while, as I worked quietly, letting my breath be the only sound I made, listening to the soft lap of the water on my ankles and rocks, the fossils seemed to . . . just show up. It got weirder: After twenty minutes, almost every stone I reached for turned out to be a fossil flipped on its side, or my hand would be drawn at the last second to a different rock than the one I was reaching for, and the new rock was a perfectly formed shell.

Was the valley doing it? I didn't know. All I knew was I had a pile of at least two hundred fossils in an hour, and when Annie came skidding back into the clearing, yelling, "I found the site!" she stopped and looked at me like I'd sprouted wings.

"Where did you find all those?" she sputtered. "There have to be three hundred!"

Three hundred? "I thought maybe two hundred," I joked. "Sorry, I'll try to work faster."

"Faster? Where did these . . . how did you . . . "

I straightened, feeling my back pop and crack as I did. "Dunno. They just sort of . . . showed up."

"Well . . . good." Annie seemed slightly disturbed. It *was* an awful lot of fossils. Like, a suspicious number. I thought the valley was having fun with us.

Or making fun of us.

"So, what were you planning to do with these again?"

"Build cairns," she said, examining some of the best specimens on the pile. "I think the boulder meadow is the best spot."

"And cairns are?"

"Oh, I'm . . . I'm sorry," Annie stammered. I wasn't sure why she was embarrassed; I was the stupid one. "They're stacks of stones. People in practically every civilization have built them to honor their dead."

"Cheerful. Why can't we just leave the pile here?"

"Oh, no," Annie said. "You'll need to carry them into the meadow. And put them into shape. We could use something to stick them together, I guess, but I think they'll hold if you stack them right. . . . "

I tried not to laugh. Annie had no idea how bossy she'd sounded. She reminded me of Carlie more than ever.

"I'll need to move them? All of them?"

She blinked at me, like I wasn't speaking English or something. "Just me?"

She blinked again. "Yes, just you. I couldn't carry all those. Anyway, I have a headache coming on." Annie sat down by the stream, fanning herself. I would have bet money she was faking it.

"Which shape?" I had a feeling I knew before she said.

"Well, pyramids."

Pyramids. I grinned. "No problem. Where do you want them, Pharaoh?"

I called her that the rest of the afternoon, until she stopped talking and really started working. She must have realized that, cancer or not, if she wanted three hundred stones moved and stacked in the next hour, she was going to have to help.

What I hadn't realized was that while I'd been collecting stones, Annie had been preparing other supplies in the meadow. She'd made . . . well, sort of small rugs out of flower petals, a different color on each boulder.

"I like the juxtaposition," she said as we stacked the fossils on top of the flower petals. "The transitory serving as the base of the eternal."

I rolled my eyes at her arty-sounding words. "Whatever. Eternal work for me, anyway."

I didn't want to talk about the art—I had a feeling I would sound dumb if I tried. But I sort of saw what she meant. When we'd finished, seven of the boulders in the meadow had carpets of flower petals—orange, red, and yellow. The fossils were stacked in near-perfect four-sided pyramids on top of each flower carpet. The gray of the stones on top of the bright colors was . . . interesting, that was for sure.

And it did make me think. About things like how long those fossils had been there, how many millions of years ago they had been alive. And how many minutes the petals had left before they would be gone, with no fossils to record them. Nothing to remember them except me and Annie and—*click!*

I turned. Annie had a camera in her hand and was taking pictures. "Move out of this shot, Peter," she demanded.

"Yes, Pharaoh," I said, bowing as I did. Had she ever heard the word *please*?

"Sorry," she said. "I get caught up. Thanks for doing this. I'm just worried. It won't last long. Not the petals, anyway . . ." She moved around the meadow, taking shot after shot of the boulders.

The cool breezes that'd fanned our faces as we'd worked had very strangely not shifted a single petal. I smiled up at the sky, wondering if the valley was watching us. First the fossils, now the breeze? Maybe the valley liked art.

I did. And it *was* art, if Annie's definition was true. I looked at it, and I saw something more than petals and stones. There was meaning there. I'd like to have spent some time sitting in it, thinking. Being still. Or even being noisy, like Annie.

Huh. I hadn't expected to have so much fun with her. I sure hadn't thought we'd make anything in the valley seem even more amazing.

"No more pictures, I'm done," I heard.

A breeze came then, blowing petals up and around me—and Annie, I saw. In a sort of tornado of petals, with funnels of red, orange, and yellow twisting around me, making the sky fill with dots of color that looked like multicolored snow. It was breathtaking, but . . .

"Annie," I said. "It's gone."

She had closed her eyes and wasn't seeing what was happening to her art. I felt sort of sorry for her. It was gone, already gone, in one stiff gust of wind.

But when Annie opened her eyes, she smiled as wide as I'd ever seen.

"You're . . . you're happy," I stammered.

"It's part of the art," she explained, motioning toward the stream. "The bringing together of the pieces, then the way they disappear when it's time—when the wind, or water, or gravity, whatever—makes the art lose its hold. It's not meant to stay forever. Some people"—she paused—"some people wouldn't get it. They'd fight to keep it. They'd do all sorts of unnatural things to make it stay just like it was. Glue it, staple it, cement it. Even though that would ruin it."

Overhead, a hawk flew, cutting the sky in two pieces. We watched it, silent together, then started walking when it had gone.

Annie's voice was low when she spoke again. "You have to learn to let go when it's time." She smiled her tight smile again, the one that had all sorts of pain and secrets behind it, and I had a dark thought in the middle of the sunny day.

I didn't think she was talking about art anymore. I had a feeling she was talking about life.

Her life.

Chapter 15

That night, my thoughts got darker. Laura had told on Dad and me as soon as Mom got back from work. I guess Laura had been bored; it wasn't like I'd done anything to her all day. I hadn't even been there to do . . . oh. The dishes. I guess Laura had had to pick up my chores. Oops.

Mom was as mad as I'd ever heard her. And considering how mad she'd been getting since Dad lost his job, that was saying something. I wished Dad *would* find a job, any job. Maybe then Mom wouldn't be so tired all the time, and worried. Maybe she'd turn back into the mom I'd had before. Mostly happy, even happy sometimes to sit still and read to me.

But she'd been way too busy for that for a long time now.

I hid out from the shouting in my room, listening to Mom scream about why her authority was being undermined and Dad yell back about her needing to loosen up.

They fought a lot these days. But never this bad . . . and this time, it was about me. My fault. Every yell felt like a punch in the stomach.

And then the fight got uglier, turned into shouts about Dad not pulling his weight and Mom being a . . . well, Dad started cussing.

He'd never cussed at Mom before.

I had to get out. Laura had locked herself in the bathroom again, with her head under the shower, it sounded like.

Carlie was sobbing in the front room, ignoring the TV, her attention on the fighting. This couldn't be good for her. It sure wasn't good for me.

Maybe Annie had been right. Maybe it *was* time to run away. But not alone.

"Let's go, Carlie," I said. "I'm gonna show you something." When I lifted her up, I noticed her diaper was a little heavy, but I wasn't about to go looking for diapers in her room—Dad and Mom might see me walk past their open door. Carlie held her arms up to me. "Peep," she said sadly. Quietly.

"Yeah," I agreed. "It is too loud here." But I knew a place that wasn't.

I hadn't counted on how heavy she'd gotten. Or maybe it was how tired my arms were from hauling fossils all day. But by the time we got to the lip of the valley, I was exhausted.

I couldn't put Carlie down, of course. She didn't have shoes on, and there were definitely snakes. "Look, Carlie," I said, to stop her squirming. The sun was setting just over the rim opposite us, and the sky was streaked with pinks, yellows, and oranges. It reminded me of the wildflowers in the valley.

"Peep!" Carlie crowed.

"Shh," I said. "Just look. Watch the light." She nodded, and I shifted her to my back so she could see—and so my arms wouldn't fall off.

We watched the sunset for a few minutes, Carlie pointing out the vultures that were flying toward a dead tree on one side of the rim and perching there. Maybe they all roosted in the same tree at night. I hoped Doug and Jake never figured out where the birds slept. I had a feeling they'd be happy to go night hunting, just for fun.

Uh-oh. I'd lost track of time. It was quickly growing dark, with a shadow from the hill framing the part of the bowl nearest us, and the shrubs and brush around us taking on darker shades. I could see fireflies flashing below us, in the valley. But none of them seemed to come up over the rim, no matter how Carlie cooed and reached out. "Dight," she said, pointing. "Dight."

"Carlie? Did you say a word?" I knew she had. She'd said, "Dight." I think she meant *light*. She'd only said names before, like "Mom" or "Peep." I'd been there to hear her first *real* word.

Cool.

"Peep?" Carlie moved on my back, uncomfortable. Or scared? "It's okay, Carlie," I said. "I'll get us home."

It wasn't that far, only a short walk back to the house. But it was dark enough that I brushed one ankle against a cactus, stubbed my toe on a rock, and almost dropped my sister when something—a bat?—flew right past my face.

At least it was quiet. Until I was a few feet from the front door, and it flew open.

"Where in the world have you been? Why did you take Carlie? What could you have been thinking?" Mom was obviously done fighting with Dad, but she wasn't all out of fight. I tried to explain that Carlie had been upset, but Mom's shouts were too loud and close together to get a word in. She grabbed Carlie and put her in the playpen. Dad was nowhere to be found. "You sit right there, Mister," Mom said, her finger shaking at me like she wished it were a gun or a stick or something more violent. "I have more than a few things to tell you about taking the safety of your family—your little sister—so lightly."

I wanted to laugh. So now Mom cared about Carlie? Where had she been when Carlie was crying with a wet diaper during their screamfest? There was a lot I could have said, but it was no use. And my headache was trying to come back. So I zoned while she lectured, thinking about the valley, and the magic there, and how—if I had my wish—I'd take Annie up on her offer, run away to it . . . and I'd never come back. Never have to be yelled at or forced to talk, to pretend I was someone I wasn't.

I knew for sure that's all I'd get at home for . . . well, forever. I just couldn't compete with all their noise, all their arguments. But if I was honest with myself, I knew the truth. I was too scared inside to yell back. To fight for being me.

When Mom finally wound down, she asked, "And what do you have to say for yourself?"

"I'm sorry," I said. The words were sour in my mouth. I wasn't really sorry at all. But I had to get away. "Can I go to my room?"

She stood there, her mouth flopping open, like she had thought I would defend myself. Like she expected something more.

"Can I?" I repeated after a few seconds.

"Yes," she finally managed, clicking her teeth shut. Her chin wobbled, like she was trying not to cry. Huh. What did *she* have to cry about? "And you think about what I said, Peter Stone. You just think about it."

"I will," I lied. Instead, I went to my room and started thinking about Annie. How brave she was, and how smart. I sort of wondered why she even liked me.

Then I remembered. Annie had been blown away by how still I could hold. But a rock could do that. I needed to show her I was smart, too. What could I come up with that might impress her? It had to be art. Something new, different, not fossils and flower petals. But what else?

Maybe something with mud, I thought, falling asleep. I dreamed of snakes made out of mud all night long, snakes that left long trails for me to follow, miles and miles of clean pathways that led me so far from home I couldn't hear any yelling at all.

Chapter 16

"Where do you think you're going?" Laura said to me in her snottiest voice the next morning. I'd slept late for once. Laura was already dressed, and she had a plate of frozen waffles in one hand. "Mom said you were grounded, right?"

I wasn't about to get into it with Laura. Anyway, I wasn't doing anything wrong. "Taking out the trash," I said, holding up the plastic bag from the kitchen. "You want to do it?" I smiled. "Sorry about the dishes yesterday."

"Dishes?" She rolled her eyes, but she was fidgeting with her hair, the way she did when she was really upset about something. "I wasn't mad about the dishes. I was scared, Peter. After last spring? You . . . you can't just vanish like that."

"Yeah, well, I won't vanish again," I said, trying not to feel guilty for worrying her. Trying not to show my surprise that she *had* worried. "Now that I'm grounded for the rest of my life, thanks to you."

She made a disgusted sound, said, "How about apologizing for stealing Carlie? Mom had a fit, and I had to listen to it," and left the room before I could even answer. After a few seconds, I heard her tapping away at the keys on the computer.

I was glad she hadn't questioned me. The bag I was holding wasn't full of trash. It was full of food.

Dad had slipped a note under my door in the night, I guess, or that morning. He was taking Carlie to try out a new daycare in Henly while he auditioned for a one-time gig playing drums at the Wimberley Rodeo. He'd be back at four. I was supposed to stay at home.

Yeah, right. I'd already stuffed enough food for breakfast and two lunches in the bag I held, along with a few more supplies. I only had to dig one more cactus spine out of my ankle that I hadn't managed to get the night before, and then I was gone until four.

I had a thought and ran back to my room. I flipped on the radio, loud enough so that Laura wouldn't check on me—she would just figure I was hanging out. But I put a note on my pillow just in case: *Went for a walk <u>on our property</u>, so don't freak. Back soon.*

And I was free. If I hurried, I'd have time to do something with the mud before Annie got there. So I ran.

I stopped on the lip of the valley, sort of saying good morning. I saw something moving across from me, two hills over. It looked like the Colonel's wife. Whoever it was held some sort of metal tool and lifted it to wave at me. I waved back and began to race down the hillside, amazed at how firm the rocks felt underfoot, how springy the soil.

It was almost like the valley couldn't wait for me to get started either.

At the streambed, I pulled out my supplies. A larger spoon from the kitchen, a metal bowl, and some of the pottery tools Mom had bought when she'd hoped my being quiet had meant I was destined for a future as a sculptor. As a surprise, in fourth grade, she'd signed me up for pottery classes. She'd let me quit after I came home with clay stuffed in my ears and nostrils, courtesy of one of the other kids who had "boundary and anger-management issues." I guess his mom had signed him up to help him control them. That hadn't worked either.

I scooped up a handful of clay, feeling it squelch between my fingers, and wondered what Mom would think if she could see me. Would she be proud of me trying to make art, real art?

Probably she'd have a fit. This wasn't really clay, after all. It was mud. And I wasn't making pots and pencil holders. Nothing useful. I was making snakes.

Well, not exactly snakes. These didn't have heads or tails. Just long, snakelike bodies. I started with one coming up out of the mud itself on the bank. Like it had been born there, formed itself from the mud. I kept going, clearing a sort of path with my sneaker toe to make a way for the mud snake across the mulch. I rolled the snake's body up and over some of the larger stones by the streambed and—seeing one of the limestone cavelets that hid the water on that side—let it disappear into the hole.

I hopped the streambed over and over as the snake wound farther away from the clay. I wished I'd brought a bucket—it was hard to hold enough mud in my hands to make more than a few inches of snake at a time. I peered up through the leaves when I thought I'd been working for a few hours. Sure enough, the light was filtering through the branches straight overhead. It was probably noon.

I stepped back for a minute to see how far I'd come. The sunlight that reached through the sheltering leaves had started to dry the mud and clay in patches, so the snake was changing color: darker brown on the still-wet places and a lighter tan on the drying lengths. It reminded me of the rattlesnake I'd seen the first day. I held still for a few minutes, remembering that day, that moment.

I think it was because I was holding still that I heard the snuffling in the grasses. I stood quietly, listening to what I was sure was a deer, coming through the brush toward the stream.

Maybe it was more than one. It made more sound than a single deer would. But when it stepped out of the brush, I saw I was wrong.

It was a hog. A black, bristly-haired wild pig, with small tusks on either side of its mouth. When it crossed to the stream to drink, it did so carefully. Was it . . . limping? I couldn't tell. It reached the mud snake, sniffed at it cautiously, and swung its head up to look around, although with those small black eyes I wasn't sure it could see much. I hoped not. Those tusks looked wicked, like it could protect itself if it needed to.

Herself. She had a low-hanging stomach and two swollen rows of teats underneath. And one foot that was swollen as well. Bitten by something, or scraped.

She was a mom. But where were her babies? The question was answered in a few seconds, as the pig let out a grunt and four small black piglets came rushing through the underbrush to join her. I was hidden in the shadows of the leaves, and I watched as they played. One of the piglets stepped onto the mud snake and left a small hoofprint there. I didn't care. It looked like a fossil. Maybe someday it would be.

One of the piglets had just wandered toward me when I heard something else. Another creature heading in our direction.

Or two creatures. *Crud.* These ones had voices I recognized.

"Hey, Doug, I think the pig came down to this stream. You get up here with the .22. I'll chase her around from the other side. She can't move fast." Jake sounded like he thought he was whispering, but every sound was amplified by the water. I understood something suddenly.

The scrape on the pig's leg—it wasn't a scrape at all. It was a bullet wound.

It wasn't right. Everything had babies this time of year, babies that would die if their mothers were killed. I couldn't let the boar be like the turkey vulture, slaughtered and thrown into a pond for fun. But there wasn't much time—the boys weren't far. I moved slightly, hoping to scare the pig away.

Bad move.

The sow bristled up, scraped the ground with one hoof, and looked like she might charge me. "Please," I whispered. "Run."

And then—I swear—the pig nodded. The babies had fled into the brush at their mom's first indication of trouble. She was gone a few seconds later, but she'd hobbled in the direction of Jake's voice. Not good.

I had to distract the guys.

"Hey, Doug, Jake. What's up?"

I wiped my hands off on my shorts and walked toward their voices. But they were there before I got a few feet from the stream.

"That you, Pete?"

"Yeah." I tried for the same tone my dad used when he had friends over. Casual, cool. I wasn't good at it. But I didn't want the boys to kill that mother pig. "You guys want some lunch?"

"Sure," Jake yelled. "Just a sec. Doug, you see her? Pete, you see a pig down here?"

"No," I lied. Then I realized there were tracks in the mud all around me.

"Dang," Jake said, stepping out of the tree cover. "We been tracking a sow since dawn. Doug shot her in the leg, we think. Wanna track her with us, Pete?" The guys were at the stream, on the other side. They leaped the water in one bound, Doug's boots slipping enough that he fell on his butt. He held a gun—a different one than the day before, bigger—up over his head as he slipped, though, like it was a baby. The water he splashed landed on the snake, and when I helped him up, his boot smashed it— but it also obliterated the hoofprints the pig had left in the mud. They wouldn't know I'd seen it.

"No, I can't. I sneaked out of my house this morning. I'm still supposed to be grounded." The guys laughed, and Jake grabbed my sack off the bank, rifling through it. He pulled out a sandwich and tore open the plastic baggie. "Thanks for lunch," he said, waving off a cloud of flies that settled immediately on the sandwich in his hand. "We had to sneak out, too."

"Why?" I watched as he threw the plastic bag into the stream. *Really?* I wanted to go grab it and put it back in the sack, but I didn't. I was going to keep an eye on these two.

Doug sat down, too, and took the other sandwich Jake handed him. My sandwich. So much for "sharing" lunch. Of course, as soon as they touched the sandwiches, flies and gnats attacked the food, crawling all over the bread even while the guys were eating. I grabbed a granola bar before they were gone, too, and settled onto a flat stone.

Doug spoke between bites. "Took my gun back. Picked the lock on the gun cabinet. Dad don't know."

"Whoa," I said. "Aren't you going to get in trouble?"

"Not if we bring back a hog," Jake said, waving a yellow jacket away from his head. "Bacon for a month, you bet." An acorn fell off the tree overhead and smacked him right below the eye, leaving a red welt.

"I hate this valley, though," he said. "We'd never have come down into it if that pig didn't already have a bullet in her."

"You shot it somewhere else?"

"Yeah," Doug said, "your house. Right out back."

They had been on our property? With guns? I had a strange thought. *Were they watching me?*

"Isn't it dangerous to shoot around houses?" I said, then realized too late that made me sound like a wimp.

"Yep, sure is," Jake said, tossing the crusts of the sandwich into the stream. "If you're a wuss. You a wuss, Petey?" He grabbed my arm and started to throw me into the water. I twisted out of his hold, but only because he slipped on some algae near the edge of the rock.

"Don't be a jerk."

"Careful how you talk to me, Petey with no gun," Jake said, taking the gun from Doug and clicking the safety on and off, the barrel pointing a little too close to my legs for comfort.

I edged away. "What?" I said, swallowing to wet my suddenly dry mouth. "You gonna shoot me?"

Jake smiled, lifted the gun, and said, "Maybe." He sighted down the barrel, and I watched his finger squeeze the trigger. I swallowed again, hard, not believing what was happening.

He *was* going to shoot me.

I froze. I couldn't make a sound, but the insects in the trees near us did, a dozen cicadas suddenly humming so loud they were practically screaming. Jake ignored them, ignored the moths and flies that flew directly in front of his view, in front of the gun barrel. As if moth wings could stop a bullet.

At the last second, he pulled the barrel to one side and shot at something behind my head.

"No shooting people, Jake," Doug said, taking the gun back. He said the words like he'd memorized them. Like it was a rule he'd had to hear over and over to get it right. To remember. Doug's eyes narrowed. "No shooting Peter," he repeated, his voice harder now as he added my name to the refrain. "I like him." Convinced that his brother wasn't about to murder me, Doug turned to me slightly. "You don't talk much. Like me."

"Wasn't gonna shoot him. It was a squirrel," Jake said. "Ran off." He looked like Doug had just taken away his favorite toy. "That hog's long gone. If we don't bring back something, and Dad figures out we took the .22, we're gonna be the ones getting shot."

I looked behind me. There hadn't been any squirrels down here when I arrived. I was almost positive he was lying.

"You shoulda seen your face, though," Jake said. He'd gone back to using my lunch supplies, fishing out the chips I'd brought and handing them to Doug. "Scared as a rabbit. You gotta get a better game face or the kids at school gonna eat you up."

"Like cake," Doug said, nodding. "Got any?"

I realized he meant in my bag. "No, sorry. No dessert." I was worried. If we stayed here too long, Annie would arrive, and if they were happy to aim guns at me, what would they do to her? She was exactly the sort of girl who got picked on by kids like this. Small, scrawny, too smart, and smart-mouthed. I had to get them out of here.

"Guys, I gotta go."

"Diarrhea?" Doug asked, matter-of-fact. "You been eatin' bad berries?"

"Um, no. I'm supposed to be grounded. I gotta get back home."

"What were you doing down here anyway?" Jake asked, scratching at some bites on his arm. "Valley of death, we told you. You're gonna get bit up, at least." He'd walked around and seen the snake I'd made. It was really long, I thought. Dozens of feet. As I watched, Jake took the top of his tennis shoes and started kicking at the dried bits, sending them sailing back into the stream. Ruining it.

I tried not to show how bad I felt, watching. "Just messing around. It's boring out here in the country." An acorn fell on my face then, but soft. *Not really*, I thought. *Not really boring.*

Jake kept on. "Also, your sister wants to know where you are. We said we'd bring you home, safe and sound, little angel cake."

I wasn't sure what to say—was he calling me a name, or quoting Laura in a sarcastic mood?

"Ugh, sisters," I said.

"Yeah, must suck," Jake said. "Although your sister's kinda

hot. I was thinking maybe she and I . . ." My stomach churned as he went on. His words seemed like they were poisoning the air.

He finished what he was saying about Laura and raised an eyebrow at me. Waiting.

I knew exactly what I was supposed to do. There was no place—city or country—where it was okay to talk about someone's sister like that. But Jake—and Doug—were both looking at me like they thought I was too much of a wimp to do anything about it.

They were right. I was a wimp. I was afraid. I'd never hit anyone in my life, even when it would have saved me from getting beaten up myself.

Beaten up again and again.

Watching the look of anticipation in Jake's eyes turn into disgust, I could hear my dad's voice in the back of my mind. Echoes from the summer before, in San Antonio. "Fight back, Peter. You've got to learn that sometimes you have to fight back. If you don't, your whole life is going to be one long series of losing—maybe more than just fistfights."

He'd put me in an after-school karate class until one of the other kids had given me two black eyes. Not on purpose, the kid had said. "Sorry, sir. He didn't even try to defend himself."

Dad had been too ashamed to look at me. He'd pulled me out of class that week.

Now, just like all those times, when I was faced with something I needed to fight, someone who was daring me to, I couldn't move. It wasn't that I didn't want to, exactly. I physically felt like I was being held in place.

Petrified by my own cowardice.

I remembered what Annie had called me the first time we met: Stone Boy. It was true, I thought. I felt like I was made of stone. Like my arms and legs were as heavy as boulders. And my heart inside was the heaviest stone of all. For a moment, I had a wild thought. I hadn't been able to stand up for myself in San Antonio, had never been able to even think about it at the end . . . but maybe here, in the valley. Maybe here I could be stronger, better.

Maybe I could at least stand up for my sister.

I made a fist with one of my hands. If I could just lift it, just move that one arm . . .

But my arm was boulder-heavy with fear. With memories of what had happened the one time I had tried to fight back, the one time I had swung—and missed.

Memories of a group of guys picking up sticks and coming at my face; memories of punches and kicks that only stopped with the sound of sirens ringing in my bleeding ears.

Still, I had to try, for Laura . . . .

And then it was too late. I'd waited too long, and my courage faded as Jake sneered. "What's wrong with you, man?" He start-ed for me like he was going to punch me, to check if I'd fight back then, but Doug stopped him with a beefy hand on his arm.

"Maybe he don't like his sister," Doug said. With his free

hand, he slapped at a horsefly that had landed on his shoulder. Jake paused, considering.

"Yeah," I said, filled with a sick relief that Doug had given me an out. Even if it wasn't true. Even if it meant betraying Laura. I swallowed a bitter mouthful of spit. "I can't stand her," I lied.

I can't stand myself. "She's the worst."

I was the worst. The worst brother in the world.

Jake looked like he still wanted to punch me. But then Doug laughed, reached down, and splashed both of us, and Jake seemed to cool off.

"She must be," Jake said. He wasn't going to hit me, but the look he gave me said I'd failed his test or something. "Sounds worse than our dad. She hit you?"

"No," I managed. "She's just . . . " I trailed off when he rolled up one jeans leg and showed me a small, round patch of skin. It looked like a burn.

"This is what happens when you screw up at our house. Count yourself lucky your sister don't smoke." I tasted bile. His dad had burned him? With a cigarette?

Suddenly, a lifetime of my dad's disappointment seemed like not such a big deal.

Then Doug tossed a rock at Jake's ankle. "Stop showing off your chicken pox scars. Let's get out of here. The mosquitoes are biting harder than piranhas."

Chicken pox scars? I didn't know what to think, who to believe. I had never seen a chicken pox scar that looked like that.

"You coming, Petey?" Doug waved me ahead of him with one hand.

I nodded, though I hadn't noticed the bugs. I'd been too busy trying to keep from hyperventilating.

A cool breeze brushed past my face, soft on my red cheeks. I hadn't been bitten, not once, but Doug and Jake looked like they were mosquitoes' favorite food. I pretended to swat at flying things the way they did, all the way up the hill. Jake and Doug slipped and slid as much as I had after I'd been mean to Annie. The valley did have ways of protecting itself.

But it couldn't do everything. I thought about the momma pig down there, trying to take care of her little piglets, bleeding from her leg. I hoped it would get better. If I could have done anything more for it . . .

No. I was weak. A coward who wouldn't even stand up for his sister.

Leaving the valley now was as close as I could come to doing anything right. Leaving and keeping these boys away from the pig. And away from Annie.

I could at least do that.

"Don't be mad, Annie," I whispered under my breath, thinking of her showing up here, spending the afternoon alone.

But alone was better than with these guys. *Hey, valley*, I thought, turning my head as we crested the rim. *Maybe next time you could do a little something more to keep these idiots out? Mosquitoes are great, but you got any mountain lions?* I was only kidding—only thinking. I didn't expect an answer. But then, on my next step, I saw the rattlesnake—it had to be the same one, it was right at the same bush where I'd seen the first one—stick its head out and taste the air, its little black tongue flickering.

And the wind whispered a hiss—*yesssssssss*.

Chapter 17

The next day, Dad took Carlie to the daycare again. Turned out, Carlie really liked playing with blocks and dolls and stuff and not just watching TV in a playpen all day. Who'd've a figured, right? Dad had noticed Carlie's crying, too, I guess. He'd even loaded up an old guitar he'd sold on eBay to get the money for the daycare. It sort of shocked me. I thought he only cared about his band stuff these days.

I was glad for Carlie. But I was stuck in the house worse than my baby sister in her playpen. Laura had gotten suspicious about where I was going. "Those boys said you haven't been hanging out with them all week. What have you been doing?"

"Hiking," I answered. Then I offered to do the laundry, her least favorite chore. I thought maybe she'd go online and get out of my hair. But it was two o'clock before Laura got tired of alternately spying and picking on me and went to join her weekly chat therapy group for teenage girls who didn't already have enough drama in their lives. Or whatever.

Once she left me alone, it felt like I could breathe again. The truth was, I couldn't even look at her without getting queasy. I felt so guilty, thinking of what I'd let the guys say about her. I had to get out of the house, get away from remembering it.

Annie wasn't at the pool, but there was a flower floating in the center of the water. She had to have gone down into the valley to look for me.

Sure enough, she was there, sitting by the stream, picking at some of the remaining snake clay with a fingernail.

She didn't look up when I got there. Mad, I guessed.

"Hey, Annie," I said, breaking the quiet. The insects stopped humming. "Did you see what I made? Well, some of it's still here. I thought you'd like it."

"You made what, exactly?" Ooh, frosty voice. Definitely mad.

I told her about my idea to make a snake out of mud that wound around the rocks—maybe even up trees—and all over the valley.

"What is it supposed to mean?" Annie said. "Art has meaning, Peter. I told you that."

I stopped talking, stunned. She'd used the tone of voice my sister used when she called me an idiot. "What's your deal?"

"Well," Annie said. "You think you made art? Tell me why it's art, then. Tell me what genius thought you had that makes this"—and she picked a chunk of snake up and pitched it across the stream—"something anyone would be interested in?"

"I don't know, exactly," I said, wondering what had gotten into her. This wasn't like Annie. She was bossy, but not . . . mean. "Something about the way this ground—the earth here—is as alive as a snake. As me." I couldn't believe I had thought this would impress her. It sounded stupid when I said it out loud.

Obviously, Annie thought so, too.

She sniffed. "Safe."

What? I wasn't sure what she meant, but it couldn't be good. I felt my ears start to burn, felt my cheeks heat as well. "Safe how? Just say what you mean."

"Easy, predictable. Safe." Annie stood up and stalked away, but I could hear every word clear as the birds in the trees around us. "It's what happens when an artist is too scared to try something new, something real. So, were you scared, Peter Stone?"

Was I scared? Why would she ask that? Unless . . .

Oh, no. Had she been there the day before? Had she heard what Doug and Jake had said about Laura, what I had *let* them say?

"You were here, weren't you?" I managed to whisper. "Yesterday. When I was down here for hours. You heard what the guys were saying to me. So you know the answer already." I felt my face burning.

She'd watched it all. And she hated me now.

"Yeah, I was scared, all right? I'm a chicken, that's all. I won't bother you anymore," I said, turning to go. "You can do your own dumb art."

My chest ached. Maybe the boys that I'd met in the valley were mean, but they were cruel to everything. Annie was only cruel to me. I'd thought maybe . . . I had made a friend.

I'd thought wrong. My throat started to close up. It was time to run away again. Not that I had anywhere to run to.

I was just about out of the meadow, wondering why I'd even bothered to come in the first place, ever thought Annie was different, when I heard one word. "Stop."

"I wasn't here yesterday," she said, and her voice sounded strange. Thick. "I didn't hear anything."

I didn't mean to listen, but my feet just quit moving. "Then why did you ask if I was scared?"

"It wasn't you. It was me."

Wait. *She* had been scared? Why?

I heard the thickness in her voice clearer now. It was tears. I turned back slowly, feeling the anger drain out of me. Annie was perched up on one of the boulders we hadn't made cairns on. Her shoulders were shaking so hard, I was afraid she might fall off.

"I'm sorry, Peter. I was being a jerk. The snakes . . . I bet the snakes were awesome. I shouldn't have said anything."

"What's wrong, Annie?" I asked. "What happened?"

"You didn't wait for me. I came after you left, I guess. Why didn't you wait?"

"I couldn't! There were these guys, with guns. They're bad, Annie. One of them almost shot me." I remembered my fear the day before, the feeling of hollowness and sick in the pit of my stomach.

"Really?" Annie wiped her face with one arm. "Who are they?"

I let out a frustrated breath. Whatever was wrong with Annie, she would tell me when she was ready. In the meantime, I'd tell her about Jake and Doug and the wild boar. It would take her mind off . . . whatever. Make it less painful, maybe.

By the end of my story—even though I left out what Jake had said about Laura—Annie was still shaking. Only now it was with rage. "That's hideous. I wish I had a gun. I'd show them how it feels to get shot."

I almost laughed. She looked like a bristly hedgehog, with her short red hair practically quivering.

"I think I got pretty close to having a firsthand experience with that yesterday," I said. "I'll stay away from guns entirely, thanks."

"I didn't figure you'd be a hunter," Annie said. "You have an artist's soul." I didn't have a chance to ask what she meant. "I'll tell you a secret," Annie continued. "I'm the scared one. I'm a . . . a coward."

"How do you figure?"

She shrugged. "I want to do something so bad, and I'm afraid."

She wanted to do something bad? Or do something *bad*? I almost laughed. "Something really bad? Get me a shovel," I said. "I'll help you hide the body."

She laughed at that. "No, not murder."

"What then?" I settled at the base of the rock she sat on, staring up at her, even though the angle of the sun made it hard to see her features. She almost glowed.

"I want to run away. For real. But I'm not sure how to make it work."

Back to that again. I guess she couldn't talk about whatever was really wrong yet. And I understood. Planning my imaginary running away had taken my mind off Mom's yelling before, so I figured it might take Annie's mind off the thing that was making her so upset now.

"Well, you've got the sleeping bag and the canteen," I said. "And the granola bars. I've got a water filter—it's only the kind that goes in the fridge, but we'll probably die from snakebite before we get *E. coli* poisoning. . . ."

"Don't make fun," she grumped. "I'm serious."

"*E. coli is* serious. But fine," I said in the same voice I used when I was humoring Carlie. "For real. What else do we need?"

She held up one hand. "A compass, I think, and definitely a knife, maybe two—" She went on and on, and I could tell she'd really thought about this. Was she serious? She couldn't be. But . . .

I interrupted her list. "No fish hooks?" I stood up so I could see her face. She was rolling her eyes at me, when I saw something more. Her arm. I walked around to the other side.

There were bruises on both her arms.

"What's that, Annie?" I pointed at one of the marks.

"Nothing," she said, tucking her arms behind her. "Just stupid camp stuff."

As far as I knew, there wasn't an activity you did at art camp that left bruises the size of fingers. "Did someone hurt you?"

"It's for the best," she said. "The other girls got mad when I critiqued their watercolors. One of them got more than mad. I bruise easily, anyway. So I told the counselor I was going to stay in my room for watercolor time."

All the anger I'd felt the day before with Doug and Jake came racing back. "How is that for the best?" Someone needed to shake some sense into those girls. Leaving bruises on a kid with cancer?

Although, come to think of it, if Annie had used that same tone of voice she'd used when she'd called me a coward, I could see how one of the campers might be tempted to leave a bruise or two.

Still, it wasn't right. "Don't they know you're sick?"

"Yeah, they do." Her voice got quiet. "And I hate it."

"Why?"

She stood up, almost shouting. "Because I'm just Cancer Girl to them. I'm not Annie Blythe, future featured artist at the Museum of Modern Art. I'm just the weird kid." She kicked a stone, and it tumbled across the ground, scaring up some small flying insects. "I hate it. Nobody even talks to me. They treat me like . . . like I have some sort of disease."

The air between us hummed with cicadas, and the words I was NOT going to let myself say.

But I did let out a small laugh. "Um . . . "

Annie laughed then, falling to the ground. "Okay, okay, I DO have a disease. But it's not contagious. I mean, it's not leprosy or anything."

I shrugged and sat next to her. "Well, you did pet that armadillo. You could have leprosy, too, by now." She shoved me, and I fell over to one side, groaning.

Annie rolled her eyes, then ran her hands through her short curls, like she was checking to see if they were still there. For a moment I realized that in not too long, they wouldn't be. The radiation—or chemo, I wasn't sure which—usually made people's hair fall out. All the girls in my class in fourth grade had grown their hair out to donate to Locks of Love, to make wigs for cancer survivors. I wondered how Annie would look with plain, boring hair like those girls. Not right.

It wasn't right.

"I'm not going to be that artist anyway," she said into the silence. "I'm never going to have an exhibit in MoMA or anywhere. I'm not going to have enough brain left, probably, to make art."

"Do you *know* that?"

"No," she said. "But I've done some research."

"On the net?"

She nodded. "Sneaking into my mom's Lucky Leuks parent chatroom, actually. She doesn't know I have her password. It turns out, when the levels are this high, for a second recurrence . . . well, let's just say that I'd better come up with any good ideas I'm going to this week. Because in a couple of months, I'm going to be relearning how to tie my shoes."

"Are you sure?" I had to ask. "Maybe you won't have any side effects at all. My mom always says to hope for the best." Of course, I hated it when she said that.

She shrugged. "*Late* effects. And to be honest? Hoping for the best is what I'm doing. I mean, I might not be able to tie my own shoes at all, right? I knew a boy at MD Anderson that happened to. Fine motor skills are one of the first things to go. Not that Mom would ever tell me about that. No, I had to find out on the freaking Internet."

"Your mom hasn't talked to you about the . . . late-effects thing?"

"Well, if you mean lied? Yeah, sure. She said it would be minor, a few months of transitioning back, blah, blah. Like last time." She stopped and cleared her throat. "But when she fought the doctors so I could come to camp, I overheard her on the phone. And then after, I saw what her friends have been telling her, what she knows is going to happen. . . . I guess she didn't want me to find out. Maybe she's right."

"Right? No." I shivered. "It's always better to know."

"Are you certain of that?" Annie sounded clinical. "I mean, if you had a disease that meant you had to get something amputated, would you rather know going in? You'd have all that time to worry, to freak out. Sort of like I'm doing right now." She laughed softly. "Or would it be better to just wake up missing your limb . . . or the use of part of your brain?"

I thought, and clouds passed overhead. Neither one of us spoke. Finally I answered her. "Better to know. Definitely."

"Yeah," she agreed. "That's why I'm sneaking. Can't trust my mom to tell me what's ahead. Of course, she's probably figured out that if I had any say in it . . . well, at least I'd still be who I am, for as long as I . . . " She trailed off, and I wondered what she meant. I thought I knew.

Annie would choose not to do the radiation at all.

Would she choose to just . . . die? Really?

I felt sick. I didn't want to think about what that meant, really didn't want to talk about it.

That would make me just like her mom. So I took a breath, wondering how to put this, wondering if there was any way I could not make it worse.

But I didn't have time to say anything. Annie stood up, wiped her hands off, and pulled me up, too. "We need art supplies. Let's go deeper into the valley and see what we find. I think I'd like to do something that takes a lot of hand-eye coordination."

"Are you . . . okay?" A seriously dumb question.

"I'm fine now. Just needed to talk that out." She forced happiness into her voice and rolled down her sleeves to cover the bruises. I wanted to ask her to stop. No matter how much we had to lie to people to get away, no matter how much we had to fake it—me faking who I was to make my dad happy, her faking how she felt about being treated like an actual leper, about being forced into a treatment no one would tell her about—down here, in the valley, honesty seemed like the only way to go.

Like it was important to be true down here. To each other and to ourselves. Even if we couldn't be true anywhere else.

Especially because of that.

Chapter 18

Two hours later, I'd climbed more trees than I'd ever imagined and stripped more dead grapevines down than I had thought could exist.

"We're making a spider web," Annie informed me when I finally had the breath to ask why we'd gathered a ten-foot-wide, three-foot-high pile of grapevines.

"A spider web?" I echoed. I wanted to ask how that was art, but thought better of it.

"Well, not today," she said. "You'll see tomorrow."

I looked up when a shadow fell. Dark gray clouds were stacking up on the rim of the valley. Rain, probably soon. It was time to go. Past time, maybe. "We'd better run, Annie, or we're going to be soaked."

If Mom saw my wet clothes, I would be in huge trouble. I heard a rumble of thunder from far off, like the sky was agreeing with me.

"Yeah, let's get back," Annie said. "I think I lost track of time." She slipped out her camera and took a quick picture of the grapevine pile.

We ran back up the hill, Annie stopping a couple of times to hold her head. I guessed her headaches were back. At the top, she waved—"See you tomorrow!"—and darted off.

I saw the figure on the hillside again before I turned to run. It was closer—and it was definitely the Colonel's wife. She was working around some trees. It almost looked like she was cutting grapevines down. Had she been spying on Annie and me? Maybe she was lonely. Maybe she wanted us to invite her to make grapevine spider webs.

"Sorry, lady, this valley isn't big enough for all three of us," I murmured into the wind.

A few seconds later, the Colonel's wife looked up, and I heard her yell, "I reckon it is. Now go home before I get it to sic the bees on ya!" The breeze rang with her laughter.

Whoa. I took a step back. How could she have heard me? And did she mean she could *talk* to the valley?

"Sorry," I mumbled, and the wind caught that, too. The Colonel's wife made a motion with one arm, like she was brushing me off, and turned back to her cutting.

I turned, too, and ran home, hoping I'd get there before my parents did.

Even though Mom always said it was best to hope, she was

wrong in this case. It would have been much, much better to stay in the valley.

❧

Mom had come home early. She was waiting at the kitchen table, right inside the front door, when I walked in. I sort of understood her worrying about me. It was raining harder than I'd ever seen it—the drops had felt more like hail than rain as I'd crossed the yard—and I was soaked.

Mom had tear tracks on her face and a wad of tissues on the table in front of her. Had she been crying about me? I wanted to apologize, but she didn't give me a chance. She just started in on the yelling.

"What has gotten into you, Peter Edward Stone? What could you have been thinking? Running off, in an unfamiliar place, without telling anyone where you were going? Worse, lying about where you were?" In her hand was the crumpled-up note I'd left for Laura: *Sleeping, don't wake me up.* This time, I'd thought to put it on my door. Unfortunately, I hadn't done much more planning beyond that, figuring that Laura wouldn't have checked on me anyway.

"Did you even stop to consider what your sister would have done up here in this godforsaken wilderness if something had happened to you?"

Godforsaken wilderness? It was the first time I'd heard Mom talk about our new home in anything other than positive terms.

"If you had gotten hurt, you could have died. We're forty miles of rough road away from the closest hospital, the phone lines were out for hours today for some reason, and our cell phones don't even work out here, for crying out loud." She shook her cell phone at me like this was my fault.

"I'm okay, Mom," I tried. I should have stayed quiet. It set her off again.

"It doesn't matter that you're okay *this* time. What about next time? Laura was worried sick about you. When she finally got a call through to me, I had to come home from work and miss two very important meetings, and for what? So you could go wandering on the hillside? Spending all that time alone—you were alone, weren't you?"

I had to tell her about Annie. Maybe she would understand. Maybe she would even help me figure out how to talk to Annie about her cancer. "No, I have a friend...." But Mom didn't even let me finish.

"Don't even think about lying to me! Laura told me what those boys said—that you haven't been hanging out at all. You didn't even go to their house."

I couldn't believe it. Why had Laura picked today to tattle on me again?

"Well?" Mom shouted, practically in my face. "What do you have to say for yourself?"

I wasn't sure she was even asking me a question. I sort of

shrugged just in case she was. I had no idea what the right answer might be.

"That's it, no more," she said. She pulled out a stack of pamphlets—brochures, it looked like—and waved them in my face. "You're too old for daycare, or trust me, I would have you in with Carlie in a red-hot minute. So it's camp for you."

"Camp?" *The brochures in her hand were for summer camps?*

"Yes, camp. Time with other kids, arts and crafts, soccer and football, camp songs. All that stuff you say you hate. I say you haven't given it a shot."

"I don't want to go." I felt my jaw hardening, clenching so tight it felt like my teeth would break. I couldn't imagine a worse summer than what she was planning for me. School was bad enough. This summer was the only time I'd ever gotten to be alone, be who I was, instead of trying to be like the rest of the world all the time.

"I'm sorry you don't want to go, but it's not negotiable. Your dad and I have been talking about this for a while. We don't have enough money for sleep-away camp, but there are plenty of day camps nearby, and heaven knows your father has enough time to drive you back and forth."

They had been talking . . . for a while? About sending me away? It sounded like something Dad would like; he'd made it pretty clear from the time I was four that I needed "fixing." Needed to be more like him. But I thought Mom . . . no. Those pamphlets had taken a while to collect. I felt my jaw click even harder. This wasn't just about today.

"You can pick which camp, but I'm done letting you waste your life. You'll end up a loner, an outcast—"

My stomach churned, but I had to speak up. "Maybe I like being a loner," I interrupted. "Maybe I'm supposed to be an outcast."

I really had to learn to keep my mouth shut.

"Maybe you could put some effort into understanding why this is so important to us! We're worried about you! And you don't even seem to care. Running off? Running away? After what you wrote last year in your journal?"

"I told you, that was just a story," I reminded her. "You said we didn't have to talk about it."

Mom's eyes filled with tears. "You wrote a story about a kid who ran away and . . . and . . . "

I stood up, and my chair fell over backward. "I *told* you, it was just a story. You shouldn't have been reading my stuff anyway." I was almost yelling. The sound made my head hurt, but at least it stopped Mom's rant.

"Peter," Mom said, her voice soft now, breaking. I couldn't stand it; it was worse than her yelling. "You know how upset that made me—all of us. We thought it was because of those boys. That's why we're here, Peter. For you. But you've been getting more and more withdrawn since we moved."

I hadn't, I wanted to tell her. Not with Annie, not when I was in the valley. It was just at home. But I couldn't tell her that. *Camp.* She was sending me to camp. If there had ever been a sign that Mom didn't understand who I was, didn't care, this was it.

"What's wrong, Peter? Do you even know?" The rain on the roof picked up speed, and the pounding overhead matched the pounding of my heart. I had to get out of there. I could feel myself collapsing, like every word she said was pummeling me like rain, like hail, and soon I would be gone.

"What's wrong?" she repeated, and the two words she didn't say were as loud as the rest: What's wrong *with you?*

I stood there, the papers in my hand feeling like a jail sentence, with Mom as my judge. She was waiting for an answer, and I knew she didn't want the truth. She wouldn't get it.

I knew exactly what was wrong. I said it, quiet but clear, before I went to my room to stay there, tearing the pamphlets into confetti-sized pieces for the rest of the night.

"I guess I was born into the wrong family."

Chapter 19

The rain kept me up that night. I think it was the rain, anyway. I heard Mom and Dad fighting again, and I woke up to what sounded like crying—Mom's. But maybe it was only rain.

The next morning, Laura was already hogging the bathroom. But she'd left a plate of cookies outside my door with a note: *Sorry.* I threw the cookies away. *Sorry* wasn't going to fix this.

At breakfast, Dad asked me if I'd chosen a camp.

I didn't even answer. I'd decided any words I used on my parents were just wasted. Just ... mouth sounds. They obviously didn't have any meaning once they left my lips, anyway. Might as well stop talking altogether.

Dad asked again. I shook my head.

"Well, let's choose now. Where are the brochures?" I went to my room, gathered the pile of confetti, and returned to the kitchen. When I scattered it on the kitchen table, Dad didn't even blink.

"Fine," he said. "I get it. You're mad. But you're going anyway. Your mom and I will choose." He smiled at his coffee. "Horseback-riding camp, maybe. I always wanted to ride a horse."

I don't, I wanted to say.

Carlie was the only one who seemed to notice I wasn't speaking. She kept yelling, "Peep! Peep!" I actually whispered a few words to her when she started to get really distressed, whimpering, "Peep!" in a broken voice that tore at my heart. But I made sure no one else was near enough to see or hear me.

And I was being watched, that was for sure.

Laura, for one thing, couldn't keep away. I think she felt guilty. "I'm really sorry, Pete," she said, looking up from the computer when I walked past. "I didn't know they'd get so mental. But it's weird, you know? We moved out here to get you away from those jerks. And it wouldn't be that hard to make new friends and get Mom and Dad off your back. There are those two boys who want to be your friends. You've just got to learn to reach out."

I did break the silence then. "You want me to have friends who steal guns from their dad and aim them at me to scare me? Actually shoot them at me, in fact? You *want* me to die?"

Her jaw dropped, and she stopping tapping away at the keyboard. "Oh my gosh, are you serious? Pete, wait!" she yelled, but

I was in my room with the door shut by the time she got to it. She could knock all day. I had no use for her. Carlie was the only one I cared about.

Well, and Annie. The rain had kept up, so I figured she wouldn't be in the valley the next day. But the day after, Friday, I was still stuck inside, Dad watching me with his patented "I don't understand Peter" expression on his face. Annie was there, I knew it, and I wasn't.

The next day was Saturday, and Mom was home. No hope.

Annie was only at camp for one more week. It wasn't fair. There was no way to get out, no way to help her make the last days before her treatment meaningful, and no one who cared enough to listen to me about why I needed to leave the house. Mom had figured out I was giving them all the silent treatment, and she told me the only words she wanted to hear were an apology for being disrespectful.

I wasn't ever going to apologize. I started dreaming about running away—not like Annie and I had been talking about, but really running away—when the doorbell rang.

Mom answered it, and I was surprised when I recognized the visitor's voice. It was the Colonel's wife. She and Mom chatted for a while, introducing themselves, and then she said, "Is that young man Peter here? Your son? I have a job for him, if he wants to earn a little money, and if you can spare him. My hands aren't as good as they used to be. Arthritis."

My mom hesitated. "Well, he's grounded."

"Ha! Grounded from helping an old lady with some grape-vines? I promise you, whatever punishment you have devised for him here, I can top it. One day with me, and he'll honestly regret—what was it he did?"

"Running off without permission. And you're right, work sounds perfect," Mom said. "And he'll do it for free. We are neighbors, after all."

She sounded positively giddy. Probably delighted to get rid of me.

I was happy enough to go, even when the Colonel's wife handed me work gloves, a pair of wicked-looking clippers, and a water bottle the size of a milk jug. "You'll need this today, boy. We've got a lot of work ahead of us." We both hopped into her go-kart. I ignored Mom and Dad, who were watching me with worried expressions. I think the go-kart had caught them off guard. Or maybe it was the helmets painted with flames.

"Never fear!" the Colonel's wife yelled as she backed out of the gravel driveway fast enough to make rocks spatter the side of the house. "I'll have him back by dinner. Maybe even with all his fingers!" She cackled as she drove off, ignoring my mom's startled "Wait!" that I could hear even above the engine's roar.

The Colonel's wife—whose real name was Mrs. Empson, she told me—wasn't lying about having work for me to do. She drove me up to the top of her hill, about a quarter mile from her house, handed me a stack of trash bags, and said, "I need you to cut every vine that isn't a grapevine. All that Virginia creeper and those sticker vines. Watch out for their thorns, they're sharp as knives—you cut them off at the base. I'd say dig out the roots, but that's no use. They're holding on to the limestone in the soil harder than a baby does her bottle."

I stared down at the clippers in my gloved hand, then at the triangular peak of her house in the distance. "All the way?"

She laughed. "Yep, all the way. Just leave the bags as they fill—I'll come by later to pick 'em up. Don't forget to drink water. I'd say watch out for snakes, but I don't think you have anything to worry about."

I wasn't sure what she meant by that. Was she referring to my boots? Or something else? But she was gone on the go-kart before I could ask. I got busy cutting. Bagging up the cut pieces was the hardest part of the job. Mrs. Empson was right about the sticker vines. They had thorns that stuck into the bags, making it almost impossible to shove them in. I ended up with scratches on my arms from trying to wrestle in the longest ones.

I don't know how long I'd worked, but I was sweating buckets. The sun was halfway up the sky, and I was wishing my mom had just lectured me to death two nights before, since at least then I wouldn't have to do unpaid, backbreaking labor for a crazy old lady all weekend, when a shadow fell over me.

"Guess I should have warned you about that poison ivy," a voice said.

"Wha—"

Mrs. Empson was standing over me, wearing an enormous broad-brimmed hat that blocked out the light so effectively I couldn't see her face. But I could hear in her voice she was laughing at me.

I looked down. The vines in my hands didn't look like the others—but were they really poison ivy? I counted the glossy green leaves on each stem. Three. Oh, crud. And I'd been holding them in my bare arms.

I dropped the bundle. "I gotta go wash this off," I said. I knew it shouldn't itch already, but the thought of how much of this stuff I'd been handling made me want to scratch myself bloody.

"Nah," she said. "You're done here anyhow, just about. You go down to Pretty Pool and wash your arms off. You won't get any rash at all."

"Pretty Pool?" I shouldered the final bag I'd cut and walked slowly alongside Mrs. Empson as we headed for her house. I was surprised at how close we were to finished—I'd done a lot of work.

"Well, I'm not sure what you and Annie—that's her name, right?—are calling it. Everybody who finds it names it something else, I reckon. When the Colonel passed and I started spending more and more time in the valley, I found it. Found out a few things about it over time. Suspect you will, too."

The smile that flitted across her lips faster than a damselfly was as mysterious as anything I'd seen in the valley. Like she knew a wonderful secret.

"Just promise you'll stay quiet. The valley don't like too much noise. I don't want to hear you caterwaulin' around down there. Sound travels, you know."

"I promise," I said. I didn't tell her I'd already promised the valley the very same thing. I didn't want her thinking I was as crazy as she was.

"Hmph," she grunted, like she could read my thoughts. "Smart aleck." She dumped her bag and mine in a pile near a barrel that looked like it had been used to burn a hundred years' worth of trash.

I scratched at my arms. "Pretty Pool," I whispered. I thought Annie's words—*effervescent* or *serendipity*—had been good. But the simplicity of *Pretty Pool* . . . it was right.

"So, you think if I wash my arms off there, I won't get poison ivy?"

She shrugged. "You never know. The valley takes care of its own. Now you help me cut these last few grapes, and I'll let you run off for the next couple of hours. I think your little friend's been waiting for you."

"Annie?" I wanted to run down now. "But . . . I'm grounded. Mom and Dad will kill me if they found out I went back there."

"What, you gonna tell 'em?" She stopped at a large wicker basket and reached for her cutters. "Humph. I got a little overzealous here. Cut a few too many already. I'll just let you carry the basket up to the house, and then you trot on off."

"Okay," I said. She'd been cutting grapes? All the ones I'd seen had been green, nowhere near ripe.

I peeked into the basket. Crazy for sure. She'd cut green grapes. They weren't any good for eating, I knew that. I guess she could do what she wanted with them, they were on her property. Or her fence line, at least. But it seemed like a waste.

"You think loud, boy," she said, breaking the silence. "Don't talk much, but you're always thinking, aren't you?"

After a second, I nodded. We'd reached the house. I wanted to step inside but glanced at my feet. "My boots are too muddy," I said.

She shrugged. "Leave 'em here. I'll wash 'em for you while you visit with Annie."

"But I need shoes," I started, then let my sentence trail off.

She was looking at me like she was going to slap some sense into me. "No you don't," she said. "You never ran barefoot down the valley? Try it. I promise. If you're what I think, then you won't get a single splinter."

Okay, weird. No matter what she said, I wasn't going to take off my boots and go running across miles of cactus, thorn vines, and snakes with no shoes on. Sure, I'd taken them off at the pool before, but only on the flat rocks. Only a truly crazy person would think of running down the hill barefoot. But I was polite enough not to say so.

What had she meant about me, "if you're what I think"?

What did she think I was?

She opened the kitchen door, a solid wood rectangle that looked like it had been made a hundred years before. The kitchen was a wreck—green grapes, glass jars, and pots and pans everywhere. I didn't say anything, but I wondered if a woman this old and . . . well, not sane . . . should be living alone.

"I like being alone," she said, even though I hadn't spoken out loud. "I like being able to decide what I want to do, when I want to do it." Her voice got crabby. "I like being able to be my own self and not have to apologize to anyone for how I am, who I am." She pulled off her hat and gave me a sideways glance. "You know that feeling?"

At first, I couldn't answer. Maybe she wasn't nuts; maybe she was psychic. She had just described the exact way I'd felt for . . . well, almost my whole life. "Yes," I finally said. "I do know."

"Run away, boy," Mrs. Empson whispered. I looked up, startled.

She cleared her throat, winked, and said, "Run off, down to the valley. I'm done with you. Come back in a couple hours, I'll get you a sandwich and drive you back home. Now skedaddle!"

She didn't have to tell me again. I skedaddled.

Annie wasn't at Pretty Pool, but I stopped long enough to dip my hands and arms in. At the last second, I splashed my face, too. It felt good, even though I wasn't at all sure it would do anything for the poison ivy I'd been handling all morning.

I was at the flower meadow in minutes. When I came through the last of the oaks, I saw someone standing with her back to me—totally still—but this girl had white, fluffy hair. Angel-soft hair, in a cloud.

When I got closer, I realized it was Annie. Her hands were fisted at her sides, full of . . . dandelion stems?

And that's what was in her hair. Thousands of pieces of dandelion fluff. Maybe tens of thousands.

"Annie?" I said, after I walked around to her front and saw her eyes were open. She was standing totally still, smiling as wide as I'd ever seen, but tears were shining in her eyes.

"Look at me," she said and giggled. "I'm art."

She was art, sort of. Transformed, anyway.

"Did you do this?" I asked. It must have taken her a while to get all those pieces of fluff in her hair.

"No," she whispered, still holding her position, not even moving her head. "I didn't." *What?* I didn't understand. Had someone else been down here with her?

"Then who . . . "

"No one," she breathed.

"How?" How had she been transformed into . . . a human-sized, enormous dandelion?

"Tell me," she said. "I don't have a mirror. Are there as many as I think?"

"Yes," I said, walking around her to appreciate just how thick the fluff was on her head. It almost completely hid her red hair. "But seriously—how?"

She giggled again. "I must be a wish girl after all. I was blowing on dandelions." She lifted one of her hands carefully. "And I was wishing *someone* would show up to make art with me. And then I closed my eyes—the wind was so soft. And I felt this start. It's been doing it for an hour, I think. I lost track."

I nodded, understanding. Wishes had a way of coming true in this valley.

"Can you get my camera and take a picture of me? I want to see it," she whispered. I reached down to her side and pulled her camera out of her bag and snapped a dozen pictures from all angles.

"Well, now what?" I said. "It looks like our art for the day is done."

"Pretty much," she said. "I have some other ideas, though. We can talk about them later. Help me blow the fluff off, okay?" She shook her head, and a hundred pieces of fluff floated down onto her shoulders and arms.

"Blow it?" I said, smiling, too. "Like you're a giant dandelion?"

She nodded. "And don't forget to make a wish."

She closed her eyes and held still as I leaned close and took a huge breath. "I wish," I said out loud—but she cut me off.

"No," she said. "Don't tell. It won't come true."

"Okay." So I made the wish in my mind.

I could hear the leaves of the trees around us start to shake and move. I took another breath, and just as I let it out, an enormous gust of wind joined me and sent the fluff that had been gathered in her hair sailing into the air in one giant burst of white, like snow.

"Wow," Annie breathed, watching the white seeds climb higher and higher into the sky. She reached up and started picking out the remaining fluffs—there were a lot—and scattered them at her feet.

"So, this valley," she said after a while. "It really is magic, isn't it?"

"I think so." I told her what the Colonel's wife had said about going barefoot and washing in Pretty Pool.

"Pretty Pool?" Annie scoffed. "What sort of a name is that?"

"Well, it's simple," I said. "But I sort of like it."

"Hmph. Pretty Pool. Not Evanescent or Lugubrious or Sempiternal . . . Pretty." She shook her head. "Plebian. But . . . fine, Pretty Pool it is. Let's go back up there. I want to swim."

"Swim?" I swallowed hard. I didn't have a swimsuit. What was she thinking?

"Might still have some of that poison ivy on ya," she teased, running ahead. "Last one there has to go in with shoes on!"

Was Annie faster than me? Normally, maybe not, but she was that day. I ran as hard as I could, but I swear the hill itself had set out to slow me down, catching my boots and toes and sending me sprawling. Though, come to think of it, even when I fell into what I could have sworn was a patch of cacti, I didn't come up with any spines.

It was the most fun I'd had in days, but Annie had to go too soon. Her mom was in Wimberley for the weekend again, staying at a nearby bed-and-breakfast. "I'll come out tomorrow afternoon," she said. "Probably late. Let's aim for four. And bring a shovel if you can."

I didn't bother to ask. Whatever Annie had in mind, I was sure it would be meaningful and transformative. Art. And if it wasn't? I had a feeling art would happen in the valley whether we made it or not.

I told Mrs. Empson not to worry about driving me home. I was feeling so full of energy after my dip in Pretty Pool, I didn't mind the walk. Plus I figured I needed to dry off before my parents saw me. "I said I'd get you back safe and sound," Mrs. Empson said, pressing a sandwich into my hand. "Don't make a liar out of me. You go straight to your house. Don't stop for nothing."

"I won't," I promised.

But I had to stop when I met Doug and Jake, at least long enough for them to beat the crud out of me.

Chapter 20

They caught me completely by surprise. I was walking slowly, since I knew I needed to dry off. When I came up the hill to my house, right before the top, I saw them sitting on the railroad-tie fence. I had a feeling they'd been waiting a while.

"Hey, Petey," Jake said. "Come here. We got to talk."

"Okay." I stepped closer, then paused. Jake didn't look good. His hair was all messed up, and he had red marks on the side of his face. Doug seemed okay, but when he walked toward me, he was limping a little.

"What happened to you guys?" I asked. It looked like they'd been in a wreck. Maybe they'd tried to go down into the valley again, and the valley had fought back, harder this time. I sort of hoped so. Maybe they'd met a mountain lion.

"You did," Doug said. "You happened, Pete."

"What?" I took a step back.

Doug's words were hard and clear. "Why'd you tell?"

"Tell?" I didn't get it. What did they think I'd done?

"I thought you were gonna be our friend." The words sounded like they hurt. The side of his mouth had a small crack and a little dried blood there.

Jake held up a hand to stop his brother talking. "Let me handle this, Dougie." He stepped right up to me, looking into my face. This close I could see that his eyes were red, too. "You told your parents about us using the .22," Jake said softly. "They came over this morning to our house. Told our dad they were worried about us having guns like that on our own. We got in trouble."

"Big trouble," Doug added.

It dawned on me that they meant they'd gotten a beating. Whoa. And I thought my parents were bad. But I said, "Guys, I didn't tell my parents anything."

"Lying won't make this any easier on you, Petey." Jake's voice was low and mean. I took a step back.

"No, I mean it. It wasn't me. I haven't even talked to my parents in days. . . . " My voice broke. Laura. "My sister," I whispered. "Laura. I'm gonna kill her."

I didn't get a chance to explain what had happened—that I'd mentioned it to Laura, and she'd obviously been the one to tell—because Doug had me by the back collar of my shirt. He might talk slowly, but he moved as fast as a striking snake.

"Here's the deal, Petey," Jake said. "Doug likes you. He

thinks maybe you don't know how to treat your friends, you coming from San Antonio and all. So we're gonna give you one more chance. We're gonna beat you now."

Beating me was giving me a chance? How was that a chance?

Before I could ask, Doug explained, "But not your face."

Oh. "That's my chance?" I started looking around, wondering where I could run, if I could make it. Even if I sprinted faster than I ever had, they were too close. I was hemmed in by the fence and the thorny brush on the sides of the road. I'd never make it out of there.

Jake shrugged. "Yeah, not your face. That's your chance—to not tell this time. So we beat you, then you're gonna go home. And keep your trap shut."

"Why?" I wasn't asking why I should keep quiet. I was asking why they wanted to beat me up, but they didn't get it.

"Because if you tell on us, and anybody—anybody—gets word that we did it, next time we won't be so nice. Next time we'll really teach you a lesson. Or maybe we'll teach your little friend one."

"My little friend?"

"Yeah, the girl. We saw you with her," Doug said. "We followed her back to camp."

Annie. Oh, no.

"She's all alone in that cabin," Jake said. "We can pay her a visit if you don't listen. But I bet you're going to listen."

And with that, he punched me as hard in the gut as he

could. It felt like he ruptured something inside. I tried to run, but Doug's hand twisted on my collar, and he punched me, too. He might as well have been using a baseball bat—he was that strong. After a few more hits, he let me go, and I fell. I curled into a ball on the asphalt, feeling kicks and punches rain down on me for the next few seconds, trying to protect my head.

I knew how to do it, how to keep my face clear. I'd had plenty of practice.

It almost felt like déjà vu. And if it hadn't hurt so bad, I would have laughed, remembering.

After school, every day, the guys in my sixth-grade class had decided to give me lessons. Private tutoring in how to take a punch to the kidney. Or a kick to the gut. I practically had a college degree in it.

They had made fun of me while they beat me up, I remembered. Called me a wimp, a coward, and worse. They'd wanted me to fight back, practically begged me to.

Dad had begged me to as well, once he suspected what was happening. "Fight back, Peter." I could hear his voice now. "You have to prove yourself, just once. Once you do, it'll stop. That's the way it works." Prove myself. To the boys, he'd meant. But also to him.

So I'd tried. Just once, a slap more than a punch. It had been a match to gasoline. The guys had taken it as permission to keep on hitting, never stop. I hadn't known they could hit even harder. I remembered the sick crack, the searing pain of one of my ribs breaking that last month in my old neighborhood. Something else had broken in me that day, something deeper.

At least Doug and Jake didn't call me names while they hurt me. I guess they knew sound traveled in the country. Or they were just more efficient at their job.

When it was over, I looked up. They were already gone, walking away like they'd forgotten I was there. Like nothing had just happened. I put a hand up to my mouth—a trickle of blood had started, I guess from when I'd bitten my tongue. But they'd kept their word: They hadn't hit my face.

I sat there crying for a while. Then I got up, slowly, hurting all over, and hobbled home.

Mom was doing the bills at the kitchen table and saw me come in. "How was your day?" she asked. Her eyebrows went up. "You look awful."

I stared at her for a minute. Thought about telling her. But I knew what she would do. She'd go ballistic, make a scene. Flashback to San Antonio, when she'd finally learned what was happening.

She'd tell their parents. Then I'd pay the price, like I had back then. The beatings only got worse when parents came into it.

And now, I had someone besides myself to protect. Annie. And Laura, or even Carlie—I wasn't sure who Doug and Jake would stop at. I had a feeling they would think all the girls were fair game.

And what would Mom do anyway? Probably just tell Dad, like she had in San Antonio. Then Dad would have to face facts again: His son was the biggest wimp in the world.

"It was hard work," I said. I thought about Doug's hammer-like fists. "Very hard."

"Good," Mom said, concentrating on her bills again. "You need to get a little stronger. Oh, and I signed you up for young leaders camp. It's sports in the mornings, public-speaking lessons and character building in the afternoons. You start in a week."

I almost laughed. Public speaking? I'd rather get beaten up by Doug and Jake for a week. "I need to shower," I said. "Take a Tylenol. And a nap." I had a feeling it was going to hurt much worse in the morning.

Mom didn't even answer. Didn't even look back up.

Chapter 21

The next morning, I slept in. By the time I got up around eleven, everyone else had eaten. I grabbed a leftover waffle and shuffled into the living room. Dad and Laura were tuning up her guitar. I hurt so bad—if I had to listen to them wail and beat on things all day long, I wouldn't survive.

"Hey, Dad," I said, peeking into the den where they practiced.

"Whoa, Pete," Dad said. "You look terrible. Did you get in a fight with a coyote?" He laughed and went back to messing with the tuner in his hand. Laura gave me a closer look, though.

"What did happen?" she asked. "Did you fall down the hill?"

"Like you care," I spat out. I couldn't tell her what had happened—or that it was because of her. She'd just tell again, and then I'd be worse off. But I didn't have to be nice to her.

"Fine, be that way," she said. "I can't wait for you to go to camp. Maybe they'll teach you not to be such a rude little weirdo."

"Laura," Dad warned. "Apologize."

"Fine," she said. "I'm sorry you're such a rude little weirdo, Peter."

"Whatever." Ignoring Laura, I interrupted Dad's guitar tuning. "Dad, the Colonel's wife—Mrs. Empson—wanted me to come back out today and finish cutting the weed vines off her fence."

"Really?"

"Really," I said, amazed at how lying to Dad had gotten so easy. I wasn't even sweating, not a bit.

Dad sighed. "You don't have to go again. It's pretty hard work for a kid. Too hard, according to your mother. She said you looked like something the cat dragged in. She was worried. You do look rough today."

"Thanks," I said, trying not to lean so heavily on the doorframe. It hurt my ribs to stand up straight. "Love the confidence."

He had to say yes. I had to get to Annie and warn her about the guys. She shouldn't be going to the valley anymore, not if they were watching her. Who knew what they'd do?

"Fine," Dad said. "You can go after lunch. Keep Carlie occupied until then? We've got to get this set straightened out, right, Laura?"

"Whatever," she said. "Let's get this over with."

§

By the time lunch was over, Dad and Laura had driven nails into my head for two hours, and I was ready to run away, even if Doug and Jake were out there waiting.

Run away. The thought kept coming back to me, over and over, as I walked away from the house and toward the valley. Annie and I had been joking about it, but now it seemed like a real option—for me, at least. Better than waiting around to be beaten, or worse.

If only there were some way to really do it. I knew where I'd run: deep into the valley. I had a feeling I'd be safe enough—from natural things, at least. But not Doug and Jake. And Mom and Dad would find me, I knew that.

Maybe if I did run, even if they caught me, they'd at least take me seriously. Maybe then they would shut up long enough to listen.

Ha. Like that would ever happen. I was pretty sure standing still and silent for even half a minute would be impossible for my parents, for Laura. Carlie had a better chance of understanding me than they did.

Even though Mom had tried over and over since I was little, she'd never really understood me. And Dad had never wanted to.

That wasn't my fault. It *was* my fault they didn't trust me, though. Dad had made me promise to have Mrs. Empson call him when I got there. Checking up on me. After all the sneaking out, I guess I was lucky he'd let me leave the house at all.

I kept feeling like I was being watched as I traveled down the road. I had brought Laura's old softball bat with me, just in case Doug and Jake decided to jump me again. It didn't make me feel safe, but it kept me from feeling helpless.

I had taken two Tylenol that morning, the only reason I was even able to stand up at all, I figured. By the time I got to the triangular red house, I felt like I'd walked a hundred miles.

The Colonel's wife met me at the door, carrying her shotgun. She set it down when she saw who it was, though.

"You walk quiet, boy," she said, like she disapproved. "I almost didn't hear you coming at all. I'm gonna have to get me a dog." She pulled a pair of glasses off a chain on her neck and perched them on her nose. "You look like heck. You fall down a mountain?"

"I fell into a cactus," I said, leaning on the side of the rocking chair by her front door. I let the softball bat fall at my feet.

"Sure," she said, looking me over. "A cactus with fists and a temper. Two cactuses, I'd say." I didn't speak for a moment, and neither did she. "So, you came back for more work," she asked at last.

"Not really," I said. "But my dad thinks so. I was hoping you could call him, tell him I got here."

"And then you'll run off into the valley? Your folks are going to get wise, boy. You should tell them." She hummed a little in the back of her throat. "You should tell them a lot of things, I suspect. Might help."

"They won't listen to me. They never do."

"Hmm." She considered, plucking at a hair on her chin while she thought. "I can't see how going down in the valley could hurt you. Or them. It's good to be out in nature. Good for the soul and the body. But I'm not going to lie for you. You want me to tell your daddy you're working for me, you're going to have to work."

Oh, no. Not more vines, I thought. She laughed.

"Thinking loud again. Here." She clomped into the kitchen and grabbed a Mason jar off the windowsill. "You go into the fourth meadow down in the valley. The one past the dinosaur tracks."

My jaw dropped. "They're really—" But she was still talking, and I didn't get the question out.

"There's a field ought to be full of rain lilies there, after that storm a couple days ago. Fill this, and bring it back. I never get down so far anymore. My back hurts too much."

"Arthritis?" I asked.

"Old hang gliding accident," she said, then hooted with laughter at my expression. I wasn't sure if she was kidding or not.

"I'll go call your dad. Get going! It's gonna be a hot one."

I got going. Annie wasn't at the stream, or in the flower meadow, or in the boulder meadow. The dandelions in the flower field had all been stripped of their fluff, and they looked . . . skeletal.

The cairns we'd made had started to crumble and fall, and the petals were all dried up and faded.

It didn't seem like a good sign. I kept going, unwilling to call out for Annie, in case Doug and Jake were down here again. I didn't trust them to wait and see if I tattled. They didn't seem like the type to control their impulses much at all.

And I didn't want to break my promise to the valley, either. I'd stay quiet as long as I could.

Maybe she hadn't come? But she'd said we were doing something special.

Then I heard something. It sounded like a dove, more than one. And someone—something else. Crying?

I walked softly around a large oak and saw her.

Annie was seated on the ground, her arms tucked around her legs, shoulders shaking. On each shoulder was a mourning dove, gray and white feathers made even plainer by the red of Annie's hair.

I watched for a little bit, until Annie must have felt me there. She looked up, and the birds flew away to perch in the low boughs of the oak.

"Hey, Annie," I said. "You all right?"

It was dumb. She was obviously not all right. But she didn't make fun of me. She just shook her head.

"What happened?" I asked, settling next to her. To my surprise, she leaned against me, like she couldn't hold her own weight up anymore. She pressed against one of my worst bruises, and it hurt, but I wasn't going to say anything. She seemed as beaten up as I'd been. My story could wait. I let the Mason jar fall with a soft thunk to the earth below.

"My mom came back for the weekend," she said after a few seconds.

"Yeah, you told me."

"So I talked to her." She hiccupped a laugh. "Yelled at her, more like. I told her I didn't want to start the radiation next week, that I wanted to wait, that maybe there's some other option. She said there *was*, actually—a clinical trial thing starting at St. Jude's in three months—but it wasn't soon enough."

"Not soon enough?"

"Well, according to her," Annie said, her voice low and rough. "And all the cancer docs in Houston, it turns out. But everybody knows they can do all sorts of amazing stuff at St. Jude's. Anyway, I asked her to call my doctor again and let me talk to him. She did, but the jerk wouldn't even listen to my idea."

"Well, if it's not safe to wait—"

"Safe?" Annie interrupted. "I'm not safe either way. So why shouldn't I wait? It's not going to matter."

"It's not?" I asked after she fell silent. "Won't the cancer get worse if you wait too long?" I didn't know much about cancer, but I knew you couldn't afford to just let it go.

"Probably," Annie said, and she sighed deep and long. "I just . . . I wish I could . . . keep going. Like I am now."

My mouth was dry, and suddenly every bruise on my body felt new, painful, sharp. What was she saying? I had to ask, make sure I understood her. "You mean, let the cancer grow?" It was almost impossible to get the words out, but this wasn't the first time she'd said something that made me think . . . I had to know. "You want to . . . die?"

"No!" Annie said, bursting into motion. She jumped up and

started pacing around the space under the oak limbs. The doves flew away in a loud clatter of wings. She'd frightened them. She'd frightened me.

"No," she said again, "I don't want to die. Not at all! But don't you see, I'm going to anyway?" She pointed to her chest. "What is death, Peter? It's when you stop being you, right? When that something, that spark or whatever, goes out. And that's what's coming for me."

"You don't know that," I protested. But she cut me off.

"I know enough. More every time I talk to her." She meant her mom. "I won't be me anymore. I won't be able to think like Annie Blythe, or talk like Annie Blythe, or maybe even dress myself anymore like—" She broke off, sobbing again.

"Like Annie Blythe," I finished for her. "But, Annie," I said, when she'd quieted a bit. "You'll still be alive. I mean, that's what's important, isn't it?"

She grabbed herself and went back to rocking on the ground. "You can't understand. I thought you might, but . . . have you ever had the people around you make a decision for you? One they don't think you can make, one they won't trust you to make? Not even the tiniest little part of it? They just tell you what's going to happen and expect you to fall in line?"

I thought about moving all the way out here. And then about summer camp. It wasn't the same, but I knew the feeling. "Sort of," I said. "Yes." My throat wanted to close up. "Story of my life right now."

Annie paused. "Tell me."

So I did. I told her about being grounded, and sneaking out, and the camp my parents were taking me to, and how Doug and Jake had beat me up—and how Mom wouldn't even listen, didn't even notice I was beaten. "Oh, Peter," Annie said, flying over to me and lifting my sleeve. She saw some of the marks there, the small cuts the asphalt had left on my skin. "I'm so sorry. I wish I could have been there. I would have—"

"No," I interrupted. "You couldn't. Those boys are mean and crazy. Annie, they know where you're staying. You need to lock your door when you're in the cabin."

"I will," she promised. "But why won't your parents listen to you?"

"They don't even like me, Annie." My eyes stung, saying it out loud. Even if it was true. "My dad's been trying to turn me into the kind of son he always wanted since first grade, when I got kicked off the peewee football team for . . ." The corner of my mouth twitched up; I couldn't help it. "For peeweeing in my uniform every time I got tackled."

She fought back a giggle. "Why the big deal? Was your dad a super athlete or something?"

I sighed. "No. I think that's the problem. He's a not-great musician who always wanted to be a star . . . something. Football player, drummer, whatever."

"Sounds like he needs therapy."

"Ha. That's what my therapist said," I muttered. Annie tilted her head.

"Your therapist? When did you have a therapist?"

"Uh, never mind." I wasn't about to start that conversation. "Leave it at this: My family thinks I'm weird."

"Well, you are," she joked. "But in the very best kind of way. All the greats were considered weird, Peter. All the very brightest—artists, scientists. They were all misunderstood as kids."

"Yeah, yeah . . ." I picked the jar back up. "Let's walk while we talk. I promised the Colonel's wife a jar full of rain lilies. Whatever those are."

She followed, muttering under her breath. "It's not right. None of it. What's happening to you and what's happening to me—it's just not fair. We're not babies. We can make some of the choices, can't we?"

"According to my parents, no. And honestly, Annie, my problems aren't the same as yours. Yours are . . . well, life-threatening."

"So are yours, Peter," she replied, her voice growing darker. "Every time your parents tell you you're not enough, not enough like them or like they want you to be—you think that doesn't kill you a little bit? It has to."

My eyes stung. She was right. And it was something I'd thought before.

"Peter?" A hand on my arm stopped me. "What are you thinking?"

"Nothing." I didn't want to answer. Then I said, "I am weird, you know."

"Weirdly amazing. Come on, Peter. You're one of the most interesting people I've ever met."

I didn't turn, didn't want her to see my eyes.

What I was thinking was that I knew exactly how she felt about wanting to be who she was. It was the same way I'd felt the year before. When I was being killed a little bit, every day, and no one would listen. Dad had told me in a thousand ways that if I would only stop being the wimp I was—the person I was—my problems would all work out. Mom had signed me up for everything she could, hoping that somehow I would change. I would be better. Different.

Annie was the first person who had ever told me I was . . . enough.

"I think you're incredible. Anybody who can't see that is . . . well, they just aren't paying attention."

When she said the words *paying attention*, an enormous blue butterfly flew up in front of my face and landed on my shoulder.

"See?" Annie said. "Even the valley agrees with me."

"You and the valley are the only ones who think so," I said, wondering at how it didn't seem crazy to think about the valley being alive anymore. Not with Annie, anyway.

"Don't you wish there was some way you could get your parents to listen to you?" Annie asked. "Something you could do to get their attention?"

It was almost exactly what I'd been thinking for two days. Maybe even two years. But nothing had worked—in fact, when they figured out how bad I was feeling, they just went and did stuff to make it worse. I nodded anyway.

"I know what to do, Peter," Annie said, rushing to me and grabbing my hands. She peered up into my face. "For you and me. To get my mom's attention and your mom's, too. To make them listen. Will you do it with me? I can't do it alone."

"What do you want to do?" I asked, feeling my mouth dry again, my heart beat faster and faster.

"Fish guts," she whispered, one corner of her mouth quirking up but her eyes deadly serious above the smile. "I'm ready."

"Fish guts?" I asked, my mind spinning. Then I remembered. "Wait. You mean . . ."

"For real," she whispered. "Let's run away."

Chapter 22

Run away . . . for real? With Annie. I wanted to yell "yes!" but my tongue wouldn't move. She waited.

"I . . . I don't know," I said, when I could speak again. I knew we'd been talking about running away, making up lists of what to take, but I'd thought it was just that: all talk. When I'd been thinking about really running away the day before, I hadn't imagined going with Annie. She was too sick. But I would never tell her that; it seemed disloyal. "Where would we go?"

"Into the valley," she said, her eyes shining. "As far away as we can get from houses."

"But . . . the valley?" I closed my eyes for a second, imagining myself in the valley, living off the land . . . and knowing it wouldn't work. Not long term. "It's big, sure. But not that big. They'd find us. Annie, you know they'd find us, and it would all have been for nothing. We'd just get in trouble."

"I know that," she said, each word slow and measured. "But

we'll be gone for long enough. Two days, three—maybe more. Long enough that your parents will shut up for good once they do find you." She started walking again, ahead of me, and I almost didn't hear her next words. "Long enough that I'll miss the start of my treatment." Her voice got lower, almost a whisper. "Maybe long enough to make St. Jude's an option."

St. Jude's? Hadn't Annie said that was three months away? Three whole months. Her doctor had insisted it was too long to wait. How bad was Annie's cancer? I wanted to grill her with questions, wanted to turn her around and make her tell me straight out what her chances of survival were if she waited— Fifty percent? Ten percent?—but I didn't.

Annie needed someone to listen. Just listen. I could do that.

So I followed quietly, wondering what Annie's mom could have been thinking. Annie shouldn't have to feel so alone, shouldn't *be* so alone out here in the countryside, with no one but a weird kid like me for company. Not when she had all this going on. Not when she and her mom should be talking, sharing the fear and pain. Not hiding from it.

Not running away.

Running away. Even the words sent a thrill through me—the thought of escaping, of being free. Being me. I remembered all the things my parents had said over the past months—years, even. About me needing to be more, better, different. Maybe they did need a wake-up call.

Maybe Annie's mom needed one as well.

It wasn't like we were really running away. We weren't going to take a train or hitchhike somewhere crazy. We'd be practically in our own backyard.

Our own very big, very wild, very magical backyard.

The idea percolated through me. If all sorts of magical things had happened at the edge of the valley, what waited farther in?

What secrets would we discover as we got farther away from home, deeper into the quiet places?

"Peter!" Annie gasped, and I raced to catch up. She had found the rain lily meadow.

It was stunning. About forty yards of nothing but white lilies, each plant no taller than a foot, with flowers about two inches across. They glistened and bobbed with the mild breeze, showing hints of purple and green when they moved. Small white butterflies, like petals that had detached themselves and decided to float above the earth, filled the sky.

"I don't want to cut these flowers." I followed a pair of butterflies with my eyes as they danced overhead. "They're too beautiful."

"I'll do it," Annie said. She took the jar from my hand and pulled a small knife out of her shorts pocket. A wickedly sharp knife, from the look of it.

"You came armed?"

"I thought we'd be cutting grapevines," she explained as she harvested a flower here, another there, taking care not to make a bald patch in the meadow. As she stepped, it seemed like the flowers bent out of her way, springing back up again after she moved her foot.

"Don't you hate cutting them?" I asked. "Flowers are so beautiful when they're growing—I've never understood why everyone wants to stick them in vases. Once you cut them, they're dead in a day or two."

Annie shrugged. "Cut or not, these'd be dead then, too."

"What?"

She rolled her eyes. "*Rain lilies*, Peter. They only bloom for one day. They're gone after that. At least the Colonel's wife will get to enjoy them like this. She deserves something beautiful in her life." Annie's voice tapered off.

"What do you mean?" I said, skirting the edge of the meadow. Annie might fearlessly tread all over the flowers, but I wasn't taking any chances on destroying what might be the most gorgeous place I'd ever seen.

"I don't know. She just seems so sad. Didn't you think?"

Sad? I would have said crazy, sure. Grumpy. Slightly sadistic, making a kid cut a quarter mile of grapevines for a sandwich. And nice, sort of, for covering for me today. But sad?

Now that I thought about it, there was something in her eyes, in the tightness around the corners of her mouth. I wondered what it was. And how Annie had noticed it when I hadn't.

I hadn't been paying attention. For some reason, the thought struck at me. Was I becoming like my family? So sucked into my own problems, I didn't notice the other people around me?

Maybe . . . maybe I needed to slow down, be more careful about my decisions.

Annie's decision gnawed at me. I couldn't even imagine . . . no. I couldn't even think about it. How could she play with her life like that? Stalling the operation and medicine she needed just to make a statement? Talk about fighting back.

I would never have that kind of courage.

When the vase was full, Annie straightened. "So, what do you think?"

"Beautiful."

Annie ducked her head. "Thanks."

"I meant the flowers," I stammered. "Not you. I mean, you are, too. Wait—"

Annie laughed, cutting me off. "Stop, Peter, you're just making it worse. But I meant, will you do it? Will you run away with me?"

"I don't think so," I said honestly. "I mean, if you run away—if we did—and something bad happened, you got hurt down there. It's really far from doctors, hospitals."

"Um, that's sort of the point," Annie said, her voice darker than I'd ever heard it. "I'm not going back to the hospital, not when they won't listen to me. Even if I have to run away a thousand times. I'm not doing that treatment."

Not doing the treatment? But without it she'd die. Wouldn't she?

I couldn't imagine it. Annie was the most alive, most energetic person I'd met in . . . well, ever.

"That doesn't make any sense, Annie," I said. I had to tell her—somebody had to. "You're talking about risking your *life*."

"Exactly," she answered, picking apart a rain lily with the bitten-down fingernails of one hand. "*My* life."

"But . . ." I had to ask. "Won't you die without the treatment? You can't just throw your life away."

"News flash, Peter. My life already got thrown away. I'm just trying to do what I want with the cruddy piece I have left."

"Annie. I never thought of you as the giving-up type."

"Don't be a jerk. I already have my quota of jerks, thanks." She threw the petals down on the ground, and as I watched, they seemed to fade and wither on the way to the earth.

I was angry, and more. But I wasn't sure who I was angry at. Myself? Her mom? Annie, for one. As much as I'd wanted to run away, her actually deciding to do it meant she really had given up hope. It meant she would rather die than try to beat the cancer again.

And the thought of that made me feel worse than I had when I was getting beat up, worse than I'd felt cutting grapevines all day, even worse than when Mom insisted on summer camp.

"You're talking about dying," I said. The words were too loud, angry, and I smelled something strange and rotten on the breeze. *Sorry*, I whispered to the valley.

"No. I'm talking about fighting back. Running away. Making them listen for once. Anyway, it's like you said. They'd probably find us before long."

"They?"

"Well, my mom, your parents. If you go with me." She faced me again. "Come on, Peter. You promised, remember? I'm serious."

Serious? I didn't even want to imagine how seriously mad my mom would be if I really did this thing.

"Your mom would be terrified," I said softly. "She probably already is. Could you . . . do that to her?"

"Yes! Maybe. Maybe . . . it'll get her attention." She sighed. "You can't understand. You probably never considered what I'm considering. You never had a problem so bad it seemed like you couldn't get away from it. Like it was a monster, chasing you, and all you could do was run."

Yes I have, I wanted to say. But the words didn't come. I didn't want to tell her what I'd gone through. What I'd been thinking of doing, no matter how many times I denied it to my mom.

I didn't want to give Annie any more ammunition.

"I've got my stuff ready," she said, her voice as steady and clear as I'd ever heard it. "I packed my backpack with everything we talked about. The canteen, the food, extra clothes—I even stole a knife from the camp kitchen."

"You stole a knife," I repeated. "You're already packed?" She'd been thinking about this, planning. "You're nuts."

"Nuts?" Her lips drew tight together. "What's the deal, Pe-ter? You chickening out?" She paused, and when I didn't answer, she went on, the words peppering me like a hail of stones. "You told me you were a coward. I didn't believe it. I guess I should have. Well, just go home then, coward. I don't need you anyway."

"Annie!" My face blazed. "Stop it!"

"Why? It's true. Either you're a coward or a liar." Tears made her words hard to understand. "Or both. You lied to me."

She was right. But I had to explain. "I . . . I never thought . . . it was all just a story, right? Like making a wish you know is crazy. It's never going to come true, so it's okay to wish for something impossible."

The air hummed between us.

"Annie, you have until Friday, right? You can talk to your mom again. Or . . . or call the doctor one more time. Come to my house, our landline works. We can go on the Internet and research some more treatments."

"I have to do something, Peter," she said after a few minutes of silence, offering the flowers in her hand to me. "You don't have to come. I'll do it alone."

Alone. When she said the word, a storm cloud, heavy and dark gray, came into view on the horizon.

"No," I said, panicking at the thought of her running off by herself. Doug and Jake might find her alone. Or she might fall, or . . . "Annie, you can't."

"I can try. *I'm* not afraid. Goodbye, Peter Stone," she said, turning to go. "Have a nice life."

She was leaving. Forever.

I watched her go, wondering if she really would do something so stupid. Wondering if I would let it happen. Wondering how to stop it.

Annie running away, maybe getting hurt or even dying . . . alone?

I had to come up with something.

I had to talk to someone who would listen.

Chapter 23

Of course, the biggest problem I had was just that: No one listened to me.

That night, I got Mom alone in the kitchen—just the two of us, if I didn't count her laptop, which kept pinging Facebook messages and clicking as she typed away.

"Mom?" I said, louder than usual. I needed her to hear me. "Mom? Can I ask you something important?"

"Um, what?" She looked up, then clued in. "Oh, yes, of course. You know you can always come to me with anything. We talked about this last year. What's going on?"

She rearranged her face to look interested, but behind her eyes was a hint of panic. Probably worried about what I'd say. Worried I was depressed again.

If she only knew.

"Well, I know this girl. . . . " I began. I didn't want Mom freaking out that I'd been hanging out with a girl all week. Too late.

"A girl?" Mom looked like I'd given her an early birthday present. "Is she cute? Where did you meet her—wait. This isn't someone you met on a chat-room online or something? You know those are all forty-year-old men, trolling for—"

"Mom!" I shook my head, wishing I'd never even tried. "She's a real girl. I've met her."

"Where?" Mom's eyes got sparkly. "When? I want to meet her. Will she go to your school next year?"

"Mom! She's not even from here. She's only here until Friday." Friday, the day her mom was going to take Annie away to start her treament.

If she could find her.

"Just . . . never mind."

"No, Peter, I'm listening. What about this girl?" She was chewing on the edge of her lip, like the words were fighting to escape any way they could.

"Never mind. We'll talk about her later." I had to try another way of finding out. "Mom, there was this friend of mine at my old school," I lied. "He had cancer."

"Who? Wait, I want to hear more about this girl you mentioned—"

"Mom, not now. This is about my friend. *With cancer.*"

Mom shook her head slightly. "I never even heard about a boy having cancer last year. Was he in your class?"

"It's not important. What I wanted to ask was, have you ever heard of late effects from cancer treatments?"

"Side effects?"

"Well, sort of. Yes. Have you ever heard of brain damage being one of them? Like, permanent brain damage?"

"Yes," Mom said, as quiet as I'd ever heard her. "I had a friend whose little boy had leukemia. He was four when they found it. He had some brain damage from the radiation and chemo. But they do therapy, you know, to help them recover."

"Do they recover?" I asked. "Let's say if someone had a lot of radiation. A lot of chemo. More than usual. If they did all that, if the cancer was serious, would the side effects be so bad she would never recover?"

"She?" Mom said. "So, is this still the girl?"

"Yeah," I said, my face going hot all of a sudden. "But not that kind of girl. What I wanted to know was—"

Mom's brow furrowed, and she hesitated for a moment, considering. "There's no way of knowing, I don't think. And that's the truth. So much about cancer treatment and recovery is uncertain. A lot of factors come into play."

I was sort of stunned. She *was* listening. For the first time since I could remember, I had my mom's attention.

"If I had cancer," I asked, "or if Carlie or Laura or I was really sick, and—"

"God forbid!" Mom stood up and started walking around the kitchen, like she was looking for something to do. "Don't say it. That's the worst thing that could ever happen to a mother. Even talking about it gives me the chills."

"But if we were really sick, and we had to do something drastic, that might cause permanent damage—and we didn't want it. Would you let us have some say? Would you let us help decide on the treatment?"

Mom stopped and whirled around. "Are you kidding? No! That's a decision an adult has to make. You can't understand when you're a child. There's nothing I wouldn't do to keep my kids alive and healthy—nothing." Her eyes were shining. "Peter, there's nothing I wouldn't do for *you*. You know that, right?"

"Even if we didn't want it done?"

Mom's mouth opened once, twice, like a fish. She reached out to hold the chair back, like she was losing her balance. "You're not—oh, God, Peter. I thought you were done thinking about that sort of thing. Have you been—"

"No, Mom," I protested, knowing where she was going. "I'm not thinking about . . . that. I never was. It was just a stupid journal."

"I know. You said that. But the things you wrote back then. And what you just said. It sounded like you meant . . ." On the desk by the computer, her phone rang. She almost turned it off without looking. Almost.

Then she glanced at the glowing screen. "Oh, crap. My boss. I've got to take this. We'll finish this conversation later, Peter. I think you might need to go back to a counselor, though. I thought it would be better out here, around new kids. Plenty of nature to keep your mind off . . . things. But it's so isolating, I can see how you're feeling. Camp . . . I hope it'll help."

And with that, she clicked the phone open before it went over to voicemail, and slipped out the door.

"What if one of your kids ran away?" I asked the empty room. "Would that be worse than one of us being sick? If we were just sick on the inside, instead of with cancer or something, then would you listen? Then would you care?"

I waited, wondering if she'd hear me and come back in.

She didn't.

Chapter 24

Wednesday came, and with it the babysitting.

"Mom," Laura had yelled that morning. "I need you to take me into town. Some of my friends are meeting up at the River Center Mall."

Mom fussed a little, but I could tell she felt sorry for Laura, being fifteen and alone in the countryside.

Me, she obviously felt nothing for. "Peter, Dad has to go to an audition at one. I'll need you to be in charge of Carlie from eleven or so until I get home."

No matter what I said—I wasn't old enough, I didn't feel safe out here with no adults—none of my arguments mattered.

I'd have to leave Annie alone again. It burned in my gut, the thought of her making life-or-death—literally life-or-death—decisions with no one to talk to. No one to convince her to change her mind.

Or to at least walk next to her.

Carlie took my mind off things for a while, with her baby talk and laughter filling the empty house. I brought her to my room and let her play with my old Duplo blocks for a while, then fed her a healthy lunch of Cheerios, applesauce, and more Cheerios.

She was almost down for a nap when I heard someone rattling the doorknob. Not knocking, just rattling. Like they were trying to get in.

Annie. It had to be her, no one else would bother—we were too far out in the sticks. For a minute, I was excited. I hadn't ever thought of inviting her to my house. Possibly, I thought, looking around at the mess and seeing the shabby paint job like it was the first time, I should have made her promise never to come out.

Too late, though. I opened the door, slinging Carlie over my hip. "Hey, Annie . . . "

It wasn't Annie. It was Doug and Jake. I tried to shut the door, but Doug stuck his shoulder out, and it was like the door hit a tree. "What do you guys want?" I asked. "I'm busy." My heart started racing. This couldn't be good.

"Busy babysitting?" Jake asked. He had a piece of Johnson grass sticking out of the corner of his mouth that he was chewing slowly, carefully. "Nobody else home?"

"Yeah, my dad's home," I lied.

Doug smiled. "No, we saw him go past. You're a good liar, though. Couldn't tell from looking at your face. I can't never hide it. We thought you'd gone, too."

Jake pushed Doug out of his way, shoving something—a screwdriver? A hammer? I couldn't tell, he hid it so fast—behind his back. "Nah, we didn't, Doug. Remember? We just came by to visit a bit. Hang out with you. Friend."

Doug look confused. "Oh, yeah," he said. "That's right. We came over to hang out."

I could see what he meant about his face giving it all away. They hadn't come over to hang out. For one thing, they hadn't knocked—they'd tried jimmying the doorknob.

For another, Doug had a big bag in his hand. Had they been coming to steal stuff?

"Can I hold your baby?" Doug asked.

I was shocked. "Um, no. She's scared of strangers." Carlie was peering at the two guys with wide, serious eyes, but she didn't look afraid, of course. She loved meeting new people. She was probably going to start smiling and babbling any second.

I was afraid, though. I didn't trust these two, especially not with Carlie.

"I won't hurt her, Pete," Doug said, each word low and sincere. "I never hurt a baby. I like 'em. They're soft."

I didn't know how to respond—soft? As in, if you squeeze

them?—and then I didn't have to say anything. Carlie had taken that exact moment to let loose a whole diaper full of stench.

Perfect timing.

"Whoo-ee!" Doug yelled, flapping an arm in front of his face. "Toxic-waste baby! You gonna have to change that?"

"Yeah," I said, acting like it bothered me. It didn't. I'd rather change a thousand diapers than hang around with Doug and Jake. "Better go soon, or it'll explode."

"Explode?" Doug hooted again, but the two of them were moving off the front step and crossing the yard. "Little land-mine baby. I like it."

"We'll see you soon, Petey," Jake said, swiveling his head back. "Maybe don't mention this little visit to anyone. Got that? We're sort of . . . grounded. Wouldn't want to have to redo the other day."

The other day. He meant when they'd beat me up.

It was a screwdriver in his back pocket, I saw, as he jogged off. And even though I could feel warmth on my arm, and Carlie was fussing, I waited there until they disappeared. Then I checked the front door.

Sure enough, there were scrapes and scratches all around the keyhole—the hole was even enlarged a bit, like he'd been jimmying it for a while. The lock wouldn't reengage, no matter how I tried. Why hadn't Dad bought a dead bolt, like we'd had in San Antonio? "We're safe out here," I remembered him saying.

"Nobody would come this far out in the country to steal. Too much work."

I guessed it wasn't too much work for Jake and Doug. I ended up stacking two chairs behind the door to hold it shut if they decided to come back, double-checked all the other doors and windows, and finally changed Carlie's diaper.

It was toxic, but not as toxic as my mood. How was I supposed to tell Mom and Dad about the doorknob without telling them who had done it?

I couldn't take another beating. And I was too much of a wimp to tell on them and risk it.

I wanted to run away worse than ever.

I found a way to tell what had happened, sort of, but it meant that I'd probably never be left alone again until I was twenty-five.

"I heard somebody at the door," I told Dad when he got home. He'd noticed the doorknob and the chairs, of course. "It was weird. Whoever it was ran off when I called out. But the doorknob was already shot."

"Shot," Dad said, running his hands through what was left of his hair. "Shot. God, just think what could have happened if he'd had a gun. And you didn't get a look at him?"

"No," I said. "I was too scared to go outside."

"Good," Dad said. He looked pale, as shaken as I had felt when I'd opened the door. "You did okay." He even reached over and gave me a hug, both his arms wrapping around me so hard I couldn't take a breath for a few seconds. "You did fine."

It was the first time in my life he hadn't criticized me for saying I was scared. I didn't know how to take it.

He spent the next hour on the phone with a freaked-out Mom, trying to calm her down. When that didn't work, he pounded on his drums until Mom got home, hammering away at them like he was going to break all the heads.

"Oh, sweetie," Mom said when she came in the door. She almost smothered me with her hug. "Where's Carlie?" She was napping, but Mom woke her up to hug her, too.

And then the fighting began.

Two minutes into the screaming, Laura rolled her eyes, said, "I quit this stupid family," and locked herself in her room. I knew how she felt. I really wished I could quit it, too.

Run away, a small voice whispered inside. *Run away with Annie.* Mom's voice obliterated any thoughts of escaping.

"Someone has to stay home with the kids until we have enough money for daycare or until school starts. It can't be me, because I'm the only one of us with a JOB!"

Mom fought dirty when she wanted to.

"So that's it? Time to start in on what a loser I am? Why didn't you just divorce me when I was fired? Why prolong the anticipation?"

"It's not too late, Joshua. Don't give me any ideas. And don't change the subject. Whatever we decide, the kids can't stay here alone so much! It's affecting Peter, can't you see it? I thought it would help, having a fresh start. But he's drawing further and further away. And even Laura's getting so lonely. You're gone so much."

"Job interviews," Dad ground out.

"Jobs are for money," Mom said. "These are for bands—free gigs, right?"

"It's temporary. I'm going to get work, so lay off." His voice had gotten harder, meaner.

"When? Before or after your kids are murdered out here in the middle of nowhere while you're farting around with your drum set in Austin like an overgrown fifteen-year-old?"

"Farting around? Come on, Maxine, say what you really mean. You know, I was a drummer when you met me—why isn't it good enough now? Why do you suddenly have this problem with who I am? Not just what I do, but *who I am*?"

I froze, listening. Dad sounded like he felt the same way I did. Like he wasn't good enough. How could he feel that way, too? I was saved from having to think about it by Mom's answer.

"Who I am?" Mom repeated, her voice high and mocking. "Because we're older, Joshua. We're adults now—or I am, at least. We have rent, bills," she shouted. "Not to mention kids, scared kids, who need someone here with them—"

"So now you want me to sit here instead of getting a job? I have to go out to find work. Peter will just have to learn to man up—"

"*Man up?* To armed robbers? Can you even hear yourself?

It's not safe! This could happen again tomorrow!"

"What, you think there's a ring of dangerous thieves going house to house in the countryside, stealing ten-year-old televisions and broken appliances?" Dad laughed, a short, ugly bark.

"There could be!"

The fight went on until they both ran out of steam. Dad finally apologized and actually figured out a few things to do to keep Mom from calling the divorce lawyers, but he had to drive into town for supplies and stay up late working with his tools to get her to back down.

The next day, he left me at home, safely locked behind brand-spanking-new dead bolts on the front and back doors and window bars on all the downstairs windows, and went around to ask the neighbors if they'd had any break-ins.

Laura was in charge of Carlie, and Mom was back at work.

I had to get out. I had to see if Annie was there. I'd spent most of the night—well, from two A.M. onward, once Laura got off the computer—doing research on late effects from leukemia treatments.

Annie had to be wrong. From what I read, the kind of effects she was talking about almost never happened. I had to figure out some way to make her see, change her . . . My own thoughts stuttered to a halt.

Make her. *Change* her. That was just the sort of thing Mom and Dad whispered about me, when they thought I couldn't hear. Or yelled, when they didn't care if I was there or not.

They wanted to change my mind, to make me see their way. Make who I was disappear and replace it with who they wanted me to be.

They never wanted to listen.

Maybe I couldn't stand up to them, but I didn't have to *be* them.

I wasn't going to do that to Annie. I was going to listen, and more. And if she didn't want to change her mind, if she was set on running away, I was going to help her do it.

Chapter 25

S he wasn't in the valley. I looked in all the places we'd been. Annie had done something with the grapevines in one of the meadows, but it looked unfinished, like she'd given up in the middle of the project.

I walked back up the hill toward the Colonel's wife's house. She was home, and her kitchen door was wide open. I could hear her humming at the sink. Her back was to me and to the table that was covered with . . . "More green grapes?" I said it out loud, and she whirled around, holding an enormous butcher knife.

For a second, I thought she was going to throw it at me. But then she lowered it and let out her breath. "Boy!" She laughed, but hard, like she wasn't sure if she was going to start yelling. "You almost gave me a heart attack."

"I'm sorry. The door was open." The room was filled with flies, and one of them landed on the tip of her nose. She blew it off, along with a few stray pieces of gray hair, and slumped down.

"Not your fault." She motioned to a stool with the knife. "Sit. You can help me strip them grapes off the stems."

I sat, and we worked together in silence for a while. The pile of grapes was enormous. And all of the grapes were unripe. I didn't get it. She was crazy, sure, but not stupid. Why had she picked these before they were ready?

It made me think of Annie, and of her cancer, and how unfair it was for a kid to have to even think about dying. Just like picking unripe grapes—it didn't make sense.

"Go ahead and ask," the Colonel's wife said after a few more minutes. "I can practically hear you thinking from here."

"What are you making?" The jars gleamed like untried experiments on the counter.

"Jam," she said. "Green mustang grape jelly. Of course, I'll have to add a whole lotta sugar to make it sweet."

"Wouldn't it be better to pick them when they're purple?"

"Well, I could wait until they're ripe," she said, "but you know, there aren't any guarantees they'll last that long."

"They might," I argued.

"Sure, but you know, the deer don't usually wait until they're perfectly ripe to eat 'em. And the raccoons, and the foxes, and all those other critters. I'd prefer to wait, but I can't. If I want grape jelly, I got to make it now, before the grapes are gone for good.

"Sometimes," she said, after a few more seconds of silence, "sometimes you got to act. You can't wait. You got to do what needs doing, before the world makes the decision for you."

There was no way she was talking about grapes.

"Has Annie been here?" I asked, wondering if Mrs. Empson knew what we were planning. "Was she here today?"

"Yep." She nodded and left it at that.

When I'd finished cleaning the grapes, she stopped me with a rough hand on my arm. I flinched; she'd hit one of the worst bruises.

"You know that mountain you fell down?" she asked. "Annie told me what really happened when she came by. Those boys are dangerous."

"You have no idea."

"Stay away from 'em, if you can. Stay in the valley, if you're not going to be at home. It'll keep you safe."

I almost laughed. "I think you're right. I wish I could live there."

She gave me a measuring look. "You know what? I imagine you could." She stressed the word *you*.

"What?" What did she mean?

"When my husband died, I went down in there. I wasn't . . . myself. The valley kept me fed and warm and dry for as long as I needed. It took me a while to get my head back on straight. More than a few weeks." She laughed. "I looked like heck, coming back up, my hair full of sticks and leaves. Like a sasquatch, I imagine."

She'd lived in the valley? "What did you eat?" I asked.

"What the valley provided," she said slowly, remembering. "Berries, nuts. Wild onions and mushrooms. Fish. Water's fresh and clean. You know, when I was down there, I kept thinking of the Bible, of the manna and quail in the wilderness. I never got a quail. Too cute to kill, I always thought. But the valley had plenty of food for me. Never did get sick off a bad berry or mushroom. I think the valley hides those from its friends."

She stopped and gave me a searching look. "But I'm not saying you should live there. Just keep away from them boys."

"I'd love to," I said, washing grapes in the giant metal colander in the sink. "But they won't stay away from me." I found myself telling her about the day before, how they'd come to the door with a screwdriver, how scared I'd been.

When I looked up, her face was white and pinched. "House robbing? That's new. Worse. Listen, son, I don't have much use for those boys' parents—there's only one place kids that young learn to be so cruel to helpless things, and that's from being helpless in the hands of bad grown-ups. But their folks got to know about this."

"Don't tell," I said, feeling a flush of terror. "They'll come after my sisters or me. Or Annie. You can't tell."

"I can't *not* tell, boy," she said slowly, like I might have trouble understanding the words. "Kids like that? If you don't stop 'em, it gets worse. Sometimes a lot worse."

"No," I said, panicked. She didn't understand. "It will only get worse if you do tell. They're testing me to see if I can keep my mouth shut."

"That's not how it works," she said. "They're checking to see if you *will* keep your mouth shut. Then they'll do worse and worse stuff. . . . I been watching them all year. They've killed most of the cats that used to live around here. People blamed it on the coyotes, but I saw them chasing after one. And now they're starting to break into places? I live alone out here. I'm afraid—"

"You're afraid of them?"

She snorted. "No, I'm afraid I'll have to shoot one of them. I don't carry my shotgun around for looks, you know."

She smiled at me, but I didn't smile back. It was no hope, I could tell. She was going to do what she felt like she had to.

"Don't say anything today," I said. "I've got to go over to Annie's camp, and I don't want them to come looking for me while I'm on my way."

"Planning to see her off?"

"Off?" What was she talking about?

"Well, her treatment got moved up. Seems the doctors were more worried about her blood work than she let on. That's why she came here—to say goodbye. Asked me to tell you the same if I saw you. She only had a few minutes to talk. Her momma's picking her up this afternoon."

I couldn't speak. This afternoon?

So there would be no running away, no getting her mom's attention. No way to change what was going to happen to her.

The injustice of it all stuck in my throat, choking me. I had finally met a friend, someone who thought my stillness, my quiet, was good, not weird. Someone who understood exactly what it felt like to be ignored when it mattered.

And now she was being taken away from me. Taken away from herself, her life, before she'd had a chance to be the incredible Annie she was obviously meant to be.

"You get on home," Mrs. Empson said, then opened the door and reached for her flame-painted helmet. "Want a ride? I'll take you, then get on over to those boys' folks. There's gonna be a stop to this, today."

"No," I said. "I don't need a ride."

She gave me a strange look, but shrugged. "Your call. Just watch out for them boys. I'll keep an eye and ear out, too. I don't think for one minute they're going to take this lying down. But if I know their folks, they won't be able to sit down for a week, or do much else."

I had to see her. Whether Doug and Jake caught me or not. I had to at least tell her I understood.

Had to explain that I'd changed my mind. That I would have

helped her run away. That I had listened to what she was saying, and understood.

✍

When I got to the camp, all the girls were inside the main barn. I could hear them singing "This Little Light of Mine," accompanied by some out-of-tune ukuleles or guitars. I had a feeling Annie would be in her bunk.

Two suitcases were stacked on the step of her cabin, teetering there like they were going to lose their balance. I thought about Annie balancing on the rocks near Pretty Pool, leaping from one limestone ledge to another on her way down into the valley next to me. After the treatment, she might not be able to balance. Maybe to walk.

My gut started churning even more. *It wasn't right.*

I knocked on the door. After a few seconds, it opened. I almost gasped. Annie had never looked so empty, so lifeless. Like she had already lost that part of her that gave her eyes their spark.

Had I hurt her that bad?

But when she saw it was me, she mustered a smile. "Hey, Peter," she said. "Come to say good-bye?"

She *was* leaving. "No, I came to—" I stopped. *To help you run away*, I wanted to say. But now . . . it was too late. "To apologize," I finished. "I didn't know you were going back today."

"Yeah, well, the doctors finally convinced Mom it couldn't wait. I go in two days early. Hooray."

She was trying to joke at a time like this? I didn't bother smiling.

"Did you tell her how you felt?" I swallowed. "Your mom. That you would rather not do the treatment?"

A short laugh. "She said I was being overly dramatic. She said it was a good thing it wasn't my decision. That I was too young and immature to be brought into those sorts of discussions."

Immature? Annie? Annie was one of the most mature people I'd ever met.

"I'm . . . I'm going to miss you, Peter." Annie's voice hitched, and I felt my own eyes fill with hot tears. "I'm going to miss making art with you. Maybe . . . maybe you'll make some on your own and send me pictures."

"Of course I will," I choked out. "But you'll come back. You'll make it with me—"

"No," she said. "I told you, I used up all my wishes."

"You don't know that. All your wishes in the valley came true, didn't they?"

She smiled, a quick turn of the lips that slipped away like a bead of water. "Well, I'm not a wish girl outside of there. I promise, I've wished a thousand times for this not to happen." She waved a hand at the suitcases.

"Where is she now?"

"Who?" Annie sat down on one of her cases.

"Your mom." I looked around. There was no sign of her mom, of any adults.

"I asked her to let me have the rest of the day to say good-bye to my friends." On the word *friends*, she made air quotes and tilted her head toward the barn. "I'm glad you came over. I only really wanted to tell you good-bye. And thanks. I've had a lot of fun with you. It was a good way . . . to end things."

No. A voice inside me roared silently. *No. Not this way. This wasn't right.*

I couldn't let her go this way.

"Tell me good-bye?" I said, when I was sure I could speak again. "Why would you want to tell me good-bye?" I felt a fierce smile stretch across my face and the pit of my belly start to lighten for the first time in days. "I mean, we are running away together, aren't we?"

Chapter 26

"We're running away?" Annie's voice squeaked. "But it's too late!"

"Why?" I felt my smile grow wider, watching the emotions cross her face—confusion, fear, amazement, hope. For the first time since Monday, I had a feeling I was doing exactly what I was supposed to. "You don't want to go now?"

"No," she said. "I mean, yes. But we have to pack our stuff—I took everything out of my backpack already. And you don't have anything with you—you'd have to go back home first. There's no time. My mom will be here in a couple of hours."

"There's plenty of time," I said, remembering what Mrs. Empson had told me. "If we're going, we should travel light. Grab a couple of water bottles, maybe a jacket. That's all."

"But food?" Annie stared at me like she thought I'd lost my mind. "Blankets?"

"The valley will take care of it," I said.

"You're nuts."

"Did you just now notice?" I answered, my grin stretching so far it almost hurt. "Let's go."

She pulled a jacket and her Doublecreek-camper water bottle out of the cabin, shoved in a couple of bags of Cheetos, and took my hand. "All right."

We sneaked around the back of her cabin, then broke into a dead run. We'd need to haul tail the whole way. A couple of hours wasn't much time. It took almost an hour to get to the rain lily meadow, and we were going much farther today.

Running across the same fields I'd cut through on my first trip to the camp, I felt thorns and stickers tear at my ankles. "Ouch!" Annie stepped on a sharp rock.

"When we reach the valley," I panted, "we won't have to worry about getting hurt."

The sun was halfway down the sky by the time we arrived at the valley's edge. It had to be four o'clock. I was hot and thirsty, but I had a feeling Annie felt worse than I did, so I let her drink all the water in her bottle. We'd stop at Pretty Pool and refill.

When we got to the lip of the valley, the wind rose up around us. "Here we are," I said. Annie grabbed my hand again, and it felt like we were about to jump off the edge together.

And somehow, I knew we wouldn't fall. The valley would catch us.

We pelted down the hill toward Pretty Pool, scaring up thrushes and grasshoppers and even a couple of rabbits. Stopping only for a few seconds to splash our faces and fill the water bottle, we raced the sun to the valley floor. Deer burst out of the brush to follow alongside us, making our feet fly to match theirs. They were close enough to touch, and I saw Annie reach out one hand to brush the dappled coat of a galloping fawn. It let her stroke it as we ran, magic on the fly.

I took it as a very good sign.

At the bottom of the valley, dusk was setting in, and we sped up, knowing we wouldn't be able to keep going once it got dark.

"Tired?" I panted to Annie when we stopped to take a quick water break. We'd refilled at the stream again, Annie joking that she'd probably die of bacterial poisoning from untreated water before the cancer got her.

I didn't laugh; it wasn't funny. But I shook my head. "The water's safe. Mrs. Empson said so."

"Did you tell Mrs. Empson where we were going, Peter Stone?"

"No. She sort of gave me the idea, though." I repeated what the old woman had said about the valley feeding me, us. Annie shook her head. "Putting your trust in a crazy person, Peter."

"I've been doing it for almost two weeks," I joked, raising my eyebrows at her.

She laughed. "How is it that no one sees how funny you are?"

"Only you think I'm funny or artistic or anything," I said, and I crossed my eyes to make her giggle one more time. "I wish

I'd known you before. Being your friend would have saved me a world of trouble. And about forty sessions with the world's most boring therapist."

Annie stopped, her hand pulling me back. "The therapist again?"

"Forget it," I said. But she just stood there, not budging. "What, you think you're the only one with problems?" I smiled so she would know I was joking. She didn't say anything, just waited. Waited until I was ready to tell my story.

I guess she'd learned that from me.

"Fine, you walk and I'll talk," I said. She started up alongside me, and I explained. "Last year, I was getting beat up by these guys in San Antonio. Like a lot, every day. At first no one believed me. These guys were the 'nice kids.' They'd even sort of been my friends when we were little. But they thought I was a wimp."

I helped Annie over a fallen log, worrying at how fast the sky was getting dark. And how hungry I was starting to feel. "Wait!" she called out. There, at the base of the log, was a huge bramble of late-ripening dewberries. "Dinner!" she said, plucking the berries as fast as she could. I helped out, amazed that the thorns seemed to bend away from my fingers as I worked. "Thanks," I murmured to the valley.

"And?" Annie prompted. "Keep talking."

"And when I told my dad, he thought I needed to work it out on my own."

"What?" Could her eyes get any bigger? Annie shook her head. "How could he?"

"To be fair, he didn't get how bad it had gotten. I begged him not to make a big deal about it. But he wanted to help somehow. So he signed me up for karate." I didn't have to tell her the karate story, I figured. This was already embarrassing enough.

"Anyway, after a few more months of getting tortured all the time—" I took a deep breath, remembering the fear, the time I tried to fight back, the broken ribs for daring to think it . . . and exhaled, letting it go. It was over. I was safe here, safe in the valley, from the pain and the memories.

"I started doing what the therapist Mom sent me to—to learn how to be more assertive, ha!—told me to do. I started journaling." I stuffed the last of a handful of berries in my mouth. "Come on, let's get a little farther in before the light's gone."

"You said you stopped writing," Annie said into the gathering dusk. "You meant the journal? What happened?"

"Mom read my journal and freaked out." I let it go at that. Maybe Annie would, too.

Of course, she didn't. "Why?" The word hung there in the air between us for at least five minutes as we jogged across meadows and around scrubby bushes and trees.

Finally, I answered her, hoping she would let the whole topic rest. "I was writing about . . . not having to deal with it anymore.

Any of it." I shook my head. "I guess you could say I'd started making plans to give up . . . permanently. On life."

"Peter," Annie said, stopping stock-still. I glanced at her face. Her eyes were shadowed and glistening. Her whole face was wet. She must have been crying the entire time I told her my story.

Crying for me. I reached up and wiped her face with my hand. No one had ever cried for me, I didn't think. Cried about me, sure, cried that I was such a loser son, such a failure.

But never *for* me.

"Peter, you were thinking about killing yourself?"

I shrugged. "Just thinking about it. I wasn't actually, you know, going to do something insane. Like run away from my life-saving cancer treatment."

Annie hiccupped a laugh and shook her head. "You jerk."

It was dark enough that I couldn't see her that well, but I felt her warm and soft as she leaned against me, into me, hugging my waist. "Peter, you should know better. You have to promise me to never think about that again. Never."

"It's not that big a deal," I said, wondering why her soft voice made my heart feel . . . whole, for the first time.

"No," she whispered. "You don't understand. Without you? I just can't imagine . . . "

She hugged me tight, and I hugged her back, wondering that anyone at all could feel that way about me. Stupid, quiet, cowardly, shy Pete Stone. The kid who had been beaten up every day for months and taken it, hidden the broken rib and the bloody noses, because fighting back—and even speaking up—hurt more.

"It's not that big a deal," I repeated, meaning that I hadn't come so close, hadn't decided anything. But she answered, "Peter, it is. Even the thought of you not being here." She sighed. "The world—the whole world—it would be so much darker without you in it. You're like . . . a light to me."

I . . . was a light?

And then, like the valley was agreeing with her, the whole world exploded into light.

At first, I was almost blinded. Dazzled. And then the light began to pulse, flash, thrum. It was—"Fireflies!" Annie murmured. "So many!"

"Where did they come from?" I asked. I almost couldn't believe it. There weren't hundreds, there were thousands. Tens of thousands. Flashing so quickly, it felt like staring at a strobe light. They lit up the ground, the area around us.

I held out one arm, and they began to land on me, covering my skin with their dark, striped bodies, their flashing luminous abdomens. I peeked at Annie; she was covered, too, giggling softly as the insects crawled over her face and hair, flying from shoulder to nose and back again. They were playing with her.

And then I heard something. "Shh . . . " I lifted a finger to my lips. Annie saw, of course—the light was that bright. But when I made the sound, all the fireflies went out.

"Annie!" I heard. "Peter!"

It was far away, very far, though the breeze that brushed our ears carried the sound clearly enough to make out our names.

These voices were somewhere near the valley, maybe not in it, but calling for us. We weren't nearly far enough away.

"Think we can keep going?" I breathed.

"Too bad we didn't bring a flashlight," Annie whispered back. And at that, the fireflies began to light up again, but this time near the ground . . . in a path. A clear, lit path looping through the brush crossing the floor of the valley. We ran for what felt like hours, following the insects' marked-out trail until we got too tired to continue—and the fireflies' lights were growing dimmer. "Sleep?" I mumbled. And then, like a wish answered, a bed of soft grass appeared, lit by the last remaining bright insects, and Annie and I both collapsed into it.

"They're looking for us," I whispered.

"Yes." Annie's voice sounded thick with tears. "Peter?" I heard in the deepening purple-black of the night. "Promise me you won't make me go back. I can't go back. I might not even remember the fireflies. The valley. You."

"Oh, Annie," I said. "I still hope . . . who knows? Maybe it wouldn't be as bad as you think. Maybe you wouldn't be lost, gone forever. Maybe you'd be . . . transformed."

"Like art?" Annie sobbed. "Oh, Peter, I wish."

I wished, too. My heart felt as heavy as my eyelids. We both knew, deep down, there wasn't any hope. They'd find us soon. In a day or two, at most. Even the valley couldn't hide us forever.

But I knew what she meant, what she needed. Someone on her side. I nodded, even though she couldn't see. "I won't make you go back. I promise."

I felt her fingers curl around my shoulder, felt her back press against my side in the soft grass. We were asleep almost before our heads touched the ground.

It was the best sleep I'd ever had. But it was followed by the worst day of my life.

Chapter 27

"I hear something," Annie said the next morning. We'd gotten up right before the sunrise, used the surrounding bushes to pee—every bit as awkward as I'd anticipated—then followed our ears to the stream. It was almost more than a stream here, practically a shallow river in places, with fish as long as my forearm swimming in some of the deeper pools. We'd eaten a nutritious breakfast of Cheetos and stream water and had a short, ridiculous conversation about the possibility of catching a fish to add to the meal. Since neither one of us liked sushi or knew how to fish without hooks, we moved on. But we still followed the stream.

"Do you think it's them?" Annie said. She'd stopped and brushed away the sparrow that had been sitting on her shoulder all morning, chirping encouragingly. It flew into a tree, and she put a hand by her ear.

"What do you hear?"

"Our parents, I think," she said. "My mom." We both held still but didn't hear anything else.

I wasn't sure about Annie, but I was starting to feel guilty. My mom was probably freaking out, having a heart attack. I hadn't even left a note. That gave me a thought. Mom didn't know about Annie, not really. The only way she'd find out was if they went to talk to Mrs. Empson.

And I wasn't sure Mrs. Empson would tell where we'd gone. She hated people in her valley. Most people. Noisy people like my family.

"Did you leave a note, Annie?"

"Um, no," she said. "There wasn't time."

"So maybe they don't even know we ran away together. Maybe they just think we're lost?"

"I'm pretty sure my mom will figure it out," Annie said. "And she won't be worried. She'll be mad. That's how she deals. Trust me, she's probably working up her lecture right now, not finding the perfect picture for a milk carton."

Ouch. Annie sounded bitter. I tried not to think about my mom, about the tears on her face when she had thought I was getting depressed again.

Well, I guess I really had been getting depressed, until I met Annie. Until I met the valley. Maybe Mom had reason to be upset.

But now I was farther from depressed than I'd ever been before. It was incredible. I could almost feel the blood running in my veins, transforming the cool morning air of the valley to energy as we walked. The breeze was full of bees and the smell of honeysuckle, and the running stream sounded like music, quiet, natural music. And my footsteps were part of the song, a perfect accompaniment. Not a triangle or cowbell in sight. I had a stray thought: I wished Dad could hear *this* music. I shook it away.

It was just like I'd thought the first day I saw it: The valley was paradise. A Garden of Eden, but real. And private.

Annie was feeling it, too. I was so glad—if she was going to have to go back—I mean, we knew they'd find us someday, and we couldn't live on berries and water forever—I was glad she had this day, this freedom, before she had to go through all that pain.

I was glad I had it, too, before I was sent off to military school or camp or whatever.

Annie ran too close to the stream, chasing a giant swallowtail butterfly, and slipped, flopping like a fish down the muddy bank and into the water. "Mud bath, Annie?" I asked. "Do we really have time for that?"

She wouldn't look at me, her shoulders shaking, and I stepped closer, carefully. Was she hurt? Crying?

No, she was tricking me. As soon as my ankle got near enough to her hand, she yanked me down into the mud with her.

There was nothing like a mud fight, it turned out, to make you forget impending hospitalization and eternal grounding.

The mud fight turned into a swim fast enough, and Annie

was good at swimming, just like everything else. Me? Not so much, and when she found out I wasn't a great swimmer, she teased me about it, throwing mud then swimming off as fast as she could.

At first, it was fun. After a while, I started to feel . . . prickly, in between my shoulder blades. Something about the way the insects were humming, or the way the birds were flying fast across the sky, like they were fleeing. The wind picked up, pulling at my clothes, like it wanted me to run with it—away, farther into the valley.

I heard something then, a yowling scream that didn't sound like anything I'd ever heard before. The hairs on the back of my neck stood up. "We're safe here," I whispered to myself. I believed it, but whatever had made that noise was big. Maybe mountain-lion big? I shook the thought away.

We were safe. We had to be. And happy, for the moment.

Bored with mud, and with me probably, since I was ignoring her, Annie swam the few feet out to a small rock in the middle of the stream, where it was deeper. Behind her, a limestone cliff went up about twenty feet, and in front of her was more of the muddy bank. She was facing me, standing up on the rock to wring the water out of the bottom of her shirt, when my neck prickled again. I saw someone standing at the top of the cliff behind her.

The sun was behind the figure, putting a halo around the shape so I couldn't see who it was. At first I thought it might be my dad or someone else looking for us, come to bring us back to safety.

But then I heard the voices—"Did you hear that? Sounded like a cougar!"—"Never mind that, I think we found him!"—and I knew. It wasn't anyone who wanted to bring us to safety. These two wanted nothing more than to hurt me—and maybe Annie, too.

How had they gotten down here? How had they found us?

Why hadn't the valley kept them out?

"Annie," I said softly, "hide."

"Why?" She splashed some water toward me.

"Hide," I repeated, frowning hard, and she paddled quickly over to the cliff, squeezing into a small recessed place that had a stone overhang. She was mostly hidden, I figured. Definitely hidden from the top of the cliff, anyway.

I stepped away from the bank. If they caught anyone, I wanted it to be me. Not Annie.

"Well, Petey, Petey," I heard. "Looks like we found you after all." It was Jake. I held a hand up to block out some of the sunlight.

I could see why I'd mistaken him for an adult. He was wearing a lot of clothes—long sleeves and jeans, a jacket, and a hat. Work boots. It wasn't his normal look.

"We been hunting for you," I heard Doug say, and I watched as his head appeared behind Jake's. He was dressed strangely, too. They both had to be sweltering hot in all those clothes. I stared as they batted bugs away from their faces, and I realized what they had done. They had worn all those clothes to protect themselves—from bugs, falls, poison ivy, all the ways the valley had of keeping them out. "We been looking all night."

As they came closer to the edge of the cliff, the wind picked up, like it was trying to push them off, tumble them into the river. But they didn't move, just stood there, watching.

"Thought you'd be down here," Jake said. "The old lady said she liked you. Told our parents we beat you up. Told them we came to your house to steal things."

"Thought you was smarter than that," Doug added. He had a stick in his hand, I noticed. A big one. Big as a baseball bat. "We warned you what was gonna happen if you told. Too bad you can't be friendly, Petey. Too bad for you."

I had no doubt about what he was planning to do. And I knew myself. Knew I wouldn't be able to fight back. Down here, so far from hospitals, from help?

They might kill me.

The cliff was long, and there was no way down. I could outrun them. The valley would make a way for me, I was sure of it.

But I couldn't leave Annie. Couldn't chance that they'd find her, alone.

"Guys, I didn't want to get you in trouble," I said. "I didn't tell. I ran away. Just let me go."

"Ran away from us, we figured," Jake said. "But there's no running away from what you got coming." He started moving forward, like he was going to climb down the cliff face and swim across for me. Doug took his stick and used it as a support to clamber down a bit further on.

A little help, I thought. *I can't leave Annie. I can't run.*

The wind picked up again, shrieking. The valley had heard me, I thought. But wind wasn't going to do it. Then I realized the shrieking was a hawk. I watched it, over Doug's head, a red-tailed hawk, plummeting faster than rain. Doug saw where my eyes were and followed my gaze, spying the hawk at the last minute. He ducked, screaming. "Jake!"

Jake stopped and ran to his brother, wrenching the walking stick out of Doug's grip and thrashing the air with it as the hawk harried them both, sharps talons only inches away from their faces. Finally, Jake threw the stick at the hawk, and the bird flew away.

At least he didn't have a weapon now, I thought, as they turned their attention back to me. And I was pretty sure the valley was going to make sure they didn't find another one.

But I was wrong.

As they came toward me, the cliff edge started to crumble. I glanced down at Annie, quickly. She had frozen there, like I'd told her. Not making a peep. But the rocks falling down were freaking her out, I could see. I moved closer to the bank, my toes squelching in the mud, ready to try and swim across to her if she needed me.

"I can run faster than you," I told the guys. "Go ahead and

climb down, but I'll be gone by the time you get here." I pointed at the rocks. "This valley hates you, but it likes me. It'll hide me as long as I need. Look—it wants to make you fall. Don't you see? All of a sudden, that cliff looks pretty unstable. If I were you, I'd back up.

"Annie, get ready to run," I said, trying not to move my lips, but the stream was so loud, I wasn't sure she'd heard me.

Just then, a rock fell down the cliff, and Annie started shaking her head. What? What was she trying to say? I was distracted and didn't notice that Doug had disappeared.

Jake called down. "You think this . . . valley . . . *likes* you? You think it's alive or something?" He hooted a laugh. "I knew you were stupid and afraid of your own shadow. I didn't know you were crazy, too."

"Say what you want," I answered, feeling my face heat. "You know this valley doesn't want you in it. But it's protecting me. Just watch. Nothing you do is going to work." I tried to project confidence in my voice, like Dad had always told me I needed to do. Tried to sound like I believed what I was saying.

I almost did.

"Get ready," I whispered to Annie, wondering what had happened to Doug, hoping he hadn't sneaked around the side of the cliff. I motioned for her to wait, but another shower of pebbles fell down, and she shook her head again, slowly moving across the water toward the small island in the middle.

"Well," I heard Doug say, then saw him reappear, carrying

something—a rock? A huge rock, at least a foot across. "Let's see what your valley can do about this."

And then he hefted the rock up over his head. The wind picked up, howling through the leaves. The sound was incredible—leaves rustling in anger, the wind screaming at the top of the cliff, the water churning suddenly, like there was a flash flood coming—and I knew I was in trouble.

I wasn't sure what was on my face, but it must have scared Annie, because she started out in earnest across the stream, swimming the remaining few feet to the rock in the middle. Doug didn't see her, I think, and Annie had no idea what was happening above her. The rock was almost in the air when Annie started to rise up on the stone island, her head moving in between me and Doug, the wet red curls on the top like a stop sign, like a warning flag.

"No," I yelled, "stop!" I was talking to Annie—but Doug listened, hesitated. And instead of throwing the rock at me with his full strength, he let it fall short.

I watched the enormous stone arc toward Annie, toward her head.

Watched it hit, saw the fear and pain on her face the split second before she fell to her knees, to her face, below the water, the red of her hair growing into a wider and longer stream of red as she bled.

It looked like she was bleeding to death.

Chapter 28

Somewhere closer than before, the yowling cry tore the air of the valley in two. "It *is* a cougar!" I heard Doug shout.

I didn't care. I didn't think about it, couldn't think about myself or Jake or a cougar or anything else. I didn't even think about Doug on the cliff, whether he had any more rocks to throw, whether I would drown trying to swim to her. I just moved.

In seconds, I was there, pulling her head above the water. "Annie!" I said. "Are you all right?"

Her eyes were shut. Was she dead? I didn't know. But I knew I had to stop the bleeding, fast. I set her head down on one of my knees. I could hold her up with the help of the water that buoyed her body. In seconds my legs were covered in blood. But then I had my shirt off and pressed against the gash on her head that ran from her temple to somewhere in the middle of her scalp.

"Oh, man, Jakey." I heard Doug's voice, but it sounded weird, high-pitched and scared. "Oh, man, it's that girl. I hit that girl with a rock."

"What girl?"

"The red-haired one. I didn't see her," Doug yelled down. "Is she gonna be all right?"

"No," I said as loud as I could with my heart pumping hard in my throat. My hands were growing bloodstained even through the fabric of my shirt. "She's not. You've got to get help."

"She's fine, I bet," I heard Jake say. I couldn't see him. It sounded like he was coming down the cliff, around the side where I'd been worried they were sneaking up on me.

I wasn't afraid of them now. There was nothing worse they could do to me than what had already happened.

Annie shifted in my arms, then slumped back down. Her motion surprised me, and I dropped the shirt to catch her, keep her from being submerged again.

The cut on her head wasn't stopping. How much blood could a girl her age lose before there wasn't any more?

I was more scared than I'd ever been. And when Jake showed up, five feet away on the muddy bank of the stream, a rock in his hand, I was the most angry I'd ever been.

"Why aren't you getting help?" I asked. "The bleeding won't stop. You two have to get help."

I watched the gleam of cruelty that usually sat behind Jake's eyes flicker, and something else take its place. Fear. For the first time ever, he looked like what he was: a ten-year-old boy. A kid, a stupid kid.

"We didn't mean to hurt nobody," Jake said. "Not really. We were just gonna scare you. We didn't even know for sure she was with you."

"Stop talking," I managed to say calmly. "It doesn't matter. Just get help. We're too far for anyone to hear us. She needs an ambulance."

When I said the word *ambulance*, Annie moaned and shifted, and the blood started to drip out the side of the shirt again.

"Oh, crud," Jake said. "We didn't mean to. I—I gotta go. Doug!" He yelled up the cliff, where his brother was scrambling down to us as well. "Doug, we gotta get. She's hurt bad."

Doug froze when he saw us. I stared into his eyes, speaking as firmly as I could. "Get help, Doug. It doesn't matter how it happened. She just needs help." I pressed my hand tighter to the wound. "I can't go. I have to stay with her, try and keep the bleeding down. *You* have to go." Why wasn't he moving? Didn't he get how serious this was? "If you don't go now, she could die."

"Die? Die? What are you sayin'? I didn't do it to kill no one," Doug said. "I never did that. I—Jake, we got to get out of here." He stopped talking and ran.

Jake gave me a scared, mean look. "You take care of her. We weren't never here. We never even saw you down here. We'll just forget the whole thing."

"What, you're going to leave us?" I managed to sputter as he turned on his heel. "You're seriously going to leave?"

Inside, a scream began to rise up, echoed by another one, closer, in the valley—the cougar.

"Run, Jake!" I heard Doug yell.

"Oh, crap," Jake breathed, then twisted around entirely and hurried after his brother. "Wait up, Doug. Wait!" he yelled, the rock falling from his hand as he fled.

I closed my eyes, so I didn't see what it was that rushed past me a few seconds later. But it smelled musky and wild, and it loped on heavy, padded feet.

After the boys. I hoped it caught them, whatever it was. They deserved it. After all, they weren't traveling in the direction of their home, of any homes. They were going farther into the valley.

They were running away. I listened as a hawk cried overhead, as their crashing footsteps disappeared into silence. Until the only sounds were water gurgling in the stream, Annie's shallow breathing, my heartbeat, and the soft whisper of a breeze in the canopy of leaves overhead.

"P—Peter?"

"Annie?" I asked. Was she waking up? She had to have a concussion. I thought I remembered something about keeping people with a concussion awake. "Stay awake, Annie."

"Hurtssss," she slurred. "Let me go."

Let her go? What was she talking about? "No, Annie, I won't. You have to stay awake."

"No ambulance," I heard her say. "No doctorsss."

I went still then, more still. What was she saying?

"You're going to be fine, Annie. You'll be okay. I'll get help."

The corners of her mouth, pale and blood-streaked, turned up the tiniest bit. "Already dying, Peter. This is . . . better. No doctors."

She slumped down again. I wanted to shake her—to wake her up, partly. And partly because I was so mad at her, I couldn't stand it.

Hot tears began to course down my face. "Annie," I whispered, feeling her slip out of my grip, feeling her weight pull her and me down the stream, like the water was trying to take her away.

I knew what she meant, but I would rather face a dozen mountain lions than hear it. Than have to watch it happen.

She wanted me to let her die. She thought, somehow, that this was a better way to go, all at once, than to lose herself to the cancer treatment.

Before, when she had told me how she felt, I had understood, sort of. She wanted to make her own decision. And she was counting on me to help her.

I had said I would. But watching her die, in my arms, I knew. She was wrong. She had been utterly wrong.

It wasn't better for her to die. It couldn't be. Already, the light in the valley was dimmer, the sounds were flat and harsh instead of magical. Already, the hum that I always felt underneath my skin when I was with her—making art, playing, just *being*—had gone still and silent.

I couldn't imagine the valley would ever be magical again without her in it. The whole world would never be . . . whole.

I couldn't imagine walking through the rest of my life, thinking there was no Annie somewhere out there. Even different, even changed, in a wheelchair, or not talking, or not remembering how to do things . . . not remembering me. All that didn't matter.

She was my friend, my true friend. The only one who had ever seen me, listened to me.

I couldn't live with myself if I let her die now.

She might never want to be my friend again. She might hate me for taking her choice away. But I had to do it. I had to break the promise I'd made just the night before.

I loved her too much to let her go.

But what could I do? I couldn't leave her, couldn't run for help.

The answer came fast: the valley.

"Help me," I whispered. "Help me, please." I held her closer, held the wet shirt against her head, her head against me, feeling the cold water grow cooler as the wind picked up.

"Help," I said again, louder. The valley wind turned sour, spat grit and leaves against my face. *I have to*, I thought, then said it out loud. "I have to!" I remembered what I'd promised the valley, that I would be quiet. That I would never ruin it, fill it with noise.

But Annie was dying, and I was the only one who might save her. I couldn't keep any of my promises. Wouldn't keep them.

I prayed the valley wouldn't send a mountain lion after me, or a wild boar, or a rockslide. I prayed it would understand.

I prayed—I wished—for it to help me. I needed to be loud. Louder than loud.

I needed to be as loud as thunder, as an avalanche, as a thousand screaming hawks.

"Help!" I yelled it. I thought about Dad's drums, Laura's guitar, Carlie's screaming, Mom's yelling, and filled myself with all that sound. Filled myself with the racket, the noise, the pain. "Help!" I yelled again, and the word seemed to echo around the clearing.

"HELP ME!" I let the words ring in my head and in the valley, bringing more noise into this magical place than I had ever been willing to, had ever thought I could.

My voice seemed to grow, louder and louder, fuller and richer and deeper, echoed over and over until the entire valley was filled with those words. Until my eardrums ached with the sound.

The words rang forever, for a thousand heartbeats, carried

by the wind. The valley was helping. My voice became as big as the sky.

But it wasn't big enough. There was no answer. Annie's face went slack, her arms dropped, stopped twitching.

It was too late.

Her breath got soft, unsteady, like a piece of dandelion fluff caught on a sleeve. Her whole body seemed to fade, grow shadowed, like a rain lily that had been picked and was starting to die.

Annie was almost gone. The light of the valley followed hers, covering us in gloom.

And then, when the darkness was almost complete, in a roar of engine and red, flame-colored glory, help arrived.

Chapter 29

"Looks bad," I heard when the engine cut off. It was the Colonel's wife.

She looked like an angel, if angels were old and frizzy-haired and fierce as any mountain lion.

I had no idea how, but crazy Mrs. Empson had managed to get her go-kart down the hill, across the valley, and up the streambed. "Like some help?" Her voice was fast and low.

"Thank you," I breathed, feeling my hands start to shake all of a sudden, like I was allowed to get weak now that someone else was there to be strong. I didn't look down at Annie, couldn't bear the thought that she might already be dead.

"Think you can hold her on your lap, keep pressing that shirt on her head?" She waded across the stream to us and lifted Annie up slowly, while I tried to keep my hands on the shirt. I slipped getting her to the go-kart, but the bleeding didn't start back up.

I wasn't sure if that was good or not. Maybe it meant there wasn't much blood left to come out. I looked down. I was bare-foot; I'd taken my boots off after our mud fight. Then I noticed Mrs. Empson was barefoot, too. She saw me looking at her feet. "Didn't have time to get dressed," she explained as she lowered Annie onto my lap and strapped us both in. "I was taking a nap, sound asleep when the wind brought your voice up to me, sent it right in my kitchen window."

"You could hear me in your house?" I couldn't believe it. We were miles away. But then I remembered the wind and the strange echoes. The valley had done it.

She nodded. "I'm pretty sure everybody in Hays County heard you, boy. It sounded like we were all in an oil drum with you. Loudest sound I ever heard." She started up the engine. "Didn't know you had it in ya."

"Me neither," I said, feeling how hoarse I was. It was the first time I'd ever felt like I'd been too loud. I stared down at Annie's head, the bloodstained shirt. I guess I had been just loud enough.

I put my face by Annie's. I could feel her breath, just barely. She was still there.

Thank you, I breathed against her skin. I wasn't sure who I was thanking, but I needed to say it.

Mrs. Empson drove us straight across the valley and up a lower hill. On the other side, there was a house I'd never seen before. A tall, gray-haired woman came out, saw us, and yelled, "Edgar! Get the keys. There's someone hurt out here."

In minutes, Annie was traveling to the emergency room with Mrs. Empson and the man in the truck, while the tall woman whisked me to her bathroom to wash up and started making the necessary phone calls. She called the camp first, then talked to Annie's mom, from the sound of it—I could hear the crying through the receiver and across the living room. Then she asked, "What's your phone number, Peter? I'll call your folks to come get you, too."

They were there in fifteen minutes, both of them, and for the first time in my life, they were quiet. Neither one spoke to me, not one word, on the drive back to the house. But the silence wasn't comforting or peaceful.

It was ominous.

"We'll talk tonight," Mom said. Her voice sounded rough, and I peeked at her face as we got out of the car. It was red, like she'd been scrubbing it. She'd been crying a lot.

Her hands were shaking as she took her purse out of the front seat, and Dad kept putting his hand on her shoulder, like he was trying to keep her from falling over.

Dad wouldn't look at me. Not even a glance. But his jaw worked constantly, like he wanted to speak but couldn't trust the words that might come out.

He waited for me to put my bloodstained shirt in the laundry, then pointed me back to my room and said, "Just stay there. Just . . . " He stopped, clenching his teeth.

In my room, I lay on the bed, thinking about Annie. Hoping

she was going to be all right. Wondering if she would ever forgive me for calling for help. Knowing I never would have forgiven myself if I hadn't.

Wishing I had had the courage to go up to the top of the cliff and punch Doug in the face before he had the chance to ever pick up a rock.

Who was I kidding? That kind of thing took guts. I'd never done anything but run away. I only knew how to hide from problems. Of course, now I was in the middle of one I didn't know how to get away from.

I heard a knock. "Come in." Laura stood there, holding a sandwich wrapped in a napkin. My stomach twisted; I hadn't eaten very much in two days, and the peanut butter smelled amazing.

"Thanks," I said as she tossed it on the bed. I took a quick bite, then asked, "Is Mom okay?"

Laura's face was raw and red, too, especially around the eyes. She'd been crying a lot. "Are you okay?" I asked, softer. She let out a sob. "I'm sorry, I didn't mean—"

"Don't act like you care," Laura interrupted, "about anyone but yourself," and she slammed my door.

I listened for the usual headache-inducing noise to start up, but for the first time since I could remember, the house was virtually silent. I could hear Carlie crying, and I wanted to come out of my room, but Dad had said to stay. So I stayed.

By dinnertime my stomach was churning, and I had learned

something new. Guilt had a taste. Like bile and sawdust and rancid peanut butter. My mouth was filled with it.

Everyone else was sitting at the table when Dad came to get me. Carlie was on Mom's lap, her face turned into Mom's shoulder like she was afraid.

I pulled my chair out and sat down. It felt like I was facing a whole group of executioners.

It felt like I deserved to be shot.

"Well," Dad said, after a few minutes. "We're listening."

I didn't know what to say. I didn't know where to start. So I waited a second, trying to come up with words that would make them see why I'd gone away with Annie.

As usual, I ended up not having to come up with anything at all. I guess my silence was the last straw for Mom.

She started crying, then, after a while, screaming, and Dad started shouting, his arm around her. I couldn't even make out any of their words; they were incomprehensible.

Incomprehensible. It was a word like Annie would have used. Long, complicated, more about the sounds you made than the meaning.

Like my family.

I thought about Annie again, about how she was going to face something a thousand times more frightening than a couple of enraged parents. I wished I could be as courageous as I wanted her to be.

I wished some of Annie had rubbed off. Transformed me.

But I was still me. The world's biggest wimp. And all of a sudden, I had the dark thought that had haunted me all of last year.

It would be easier if I disappeared. If I gave up.

If I died.

No. I felt something jerk inside, in my mind, my heart. I had promised Annie I would never even think that. I wasn't going to break that promise.

"No," I whispered, and it seemed like Annie's voice was there, too, echoing mine. Maybe I had been transformed.

My mouth opened on its own, like my body was trying to help me. My feet shifted under the table. Suddenly, I knew what I had to say. I just didn't know if I had the courage to say it.

I stood up, slowly, and held up a hand. Like magic, they all got quiet.

"I can't tell you what you want to hear," I said, hoping they would understand that, in my own way, I was answering them. "I can't. I gave that up a long time ago." I took a breath, realizing that they were finally listening. "I gave up on me. I gave up a while back. Back when I was writing about . . . dying."

"But we took you away from all that, from them," Mom said after a few seconds, a dozen heartbeats. "Those boys who were hurting you—"

I held my hand up again. "Yes," I said slowly. "But they weren't why I wanted to . . . disappear. Why I was thinking about . . . disappearing."

I took another breath, fear filling my chest. "*You* were."

"Why?" Mom said, horrified, and stopped. No one spoke.

My hand was shaking so hard I could see it. I folded my trembling fingers and started again. "I thought for months about how to make you see . . . ways to show you. But you're never quiet long enough for me to tell you what I'm thinking. No one listens to me. And I can't even think when I'm here."

"Here?" Dad said. His voice was shaky, strange. "Home, you mean?"

I nodded. "Around you. It's the noise. I can't even think when it all starts. And pretty soon, disappearing seems like the best—"

"What are you talking about?" Laura broke in. "What could we have possibly done to make you think about those things, to make you run away? With a stranger!" Her voice was rough, like Mom's. She was crying again. I thought she was going to start yelling, like usual, but Mom put a hand on her arm and a finger to her lips. "Shh."

And Laura stopped. "Okay," she said and hiccupped, sniffling as she looked down at the table. "I'm listening."

"I ran away with Annie because she *heard* me. She thought I was special. In a good way," I said, smiling at Laura. She didn't smile back. "She understood who I was from the first time she met me."

"More than your family?" Dad's words fell heavy into the room, like each one was tied to a rock that landed against my throat. I closed my eyes to answer; I couldn't look at his face.

"Camps. Karate. Public speaking. Football. Every time you

put me in those things, against my will, you might as well have yelled at me: 'You're not enough, Peter.' It hurt me worse than all the beatings I took. I've known all my life I wasn't who you wanted me to be. I knew I never would be."

Dad's voice sounded like he'd swallowed glass. "Peter, you got it wrong. I never wanted to hurt you. I never knew what to do to help you—" He broke off, swallowing hard. "I love you, son. I only wanted what was best."

"What you thought was best." I stared right at him. He had to understand. "What would have made *you* feel better about me. Not what I needed."

I fought past the bruised feeling in my throat, in my memories. "Annie listened to me, Dad. She didn't try to change me into who she wanted me to be, like . . . like you do. She thought I was good enough already. Like I am. Who I am. She made me feel like I was worth something. I'd never felt that before."

My mom dissolved into quiet tears. It felt like a fist was squeezing my heart. "Mom, I'm sorry. I didn't mean—"

"No," she said. "It's okay. I'm listening now. We're listening. Keep talking."

I couldn't keep talking. Each word was a weight. But I had to try. "The first time I ran away, I found this place where I was happy for the first time in years, more than happy. This valley. It's . . . " I stopped. "I can't explain. When I'm there, I can be myself."

Carlie had slipped down from her high chair and toddled

over to my leg, but she wasn't making a single noise. She was holding still. I had an idea.

"Can I show you, Dad?" I asked. "Who I am?"

It was what he had said to Mom a few nights before, while they were fighting. He remembered it, I could tell. So did Mom. She was crying harder now and had crumpled, sort of, folded down into herself like a wilted rain lily. Dad murmured her name like a question—"Maxine?"—and she shook her head, not looking up.

I stared into Dad's eyes. For the first time I could remember, he was looking at me like he saw something worth noticing. Like he really saw me—not a defective copy of himself.

"Please. Can I show you—all of you—who I am?"

I was out of words. I'd spoken more in the last ten minutes than I had in the last ten months. I waited.

No one spoke at first. But after a few seconds, they all nodded, except Carlie, who held up her arms and whispered, "Peep."

I picked her up and took my family to the one place I'd decided I would never let them see. The one place I was sure they'd ruin if I let them anywhere near it.

When we got there, the wind started up, the steady breeze that always blew from the valley to greet me. This time, it brushed my face like a question.

I held my breath, hoping my family would listen, would feel it, the way I had. Hoping against hope they would understand what it was I was trying to show them.

Carlie shifted and leaned into my chest. "Dight," she said.

"Soon," I breathed back. The light was fading already, and I knew the lightning bugs would come out in the next hour. If I could get them to stay with me that long . . .

"What do we do?" Mom whispered, coming up next to me. She was breathing slowly now, and I realized her steady breath against my hair reminded me of the wind in the valley, the way it would brush against me when Annie and I had been making art.

"Just listen," I said. "And be still."

"For how long?" Dad murmured, his hand on my shoulder.

I didn't answer, just breathed in. Laura sat down near my feet, staring across the valley. The sun was just slipping down across the rim of hills, and the sky was changing from the magentas and oranges of sunset to the dark purple-blues of twilight.

"It's so beautiful," Laura said.

Carlie put her finger to her lips. "Shh."

I would never have believed they could do it, but they did. My whole family held as still as statues—as still as I did, almost. We watched the wind start across the valley, blowing tree branches like blades of grass. It shifted over the edge of the hill at our feet, hesitant.

But no one moved, no one spoke. Then Carlie pointed one chubby finger up.

It was like a conductor had lifted a baton. As her arm came down, the chorus frogs started peeping all around us, their trills echoing until it seemed like there were a million of them. A whippoorwill called across the hill and another one answered, back and forth, until they were calling out to each other, a counterpoint to the frogs.

An owl sang out, and the lap of water on stone inexplicably sailed all the way from Pretty Pool to my ears, calling me.

I shook my head. My mother had wrapped her hand in mine and was holding on tight, like she was afraid she might be swept away by the breeze. I peeked at her face; it was shining with tears . . . but she was smiling as wide as I'd ever seen.

And Dad was smiling right next to her. They were holding hands, too. I hadn't seen them do that in years.

The night became music, with owls and more nightjars adding their notes to the chorus . . . and then the light show began.

The valley was showing off. I thought I'd seen a lot of fireflies before, with Annie. But now, the whole valley seemed to come to life, the fireflies blinking and moving like circling constellations below us, echoing the real ones that had begun to appear above.

"Dight," Carlie whispered, pointing. "Dight."

The fireflies came dancing up from the valley floor in great spirals, in looping ribbons of light. For a moment, I almost thought the ribbon spelled out Annie's name—but then the fireflies were there, with us, surrounding us. They landed on me—on Carlie, too, and Mom and Dad and Laura—sparkling like lighted jewels until we all four shone and twinkled.

Like we were stars ourselves, bits of stardust, fallen to earth.

"It's magic," Laura sighed.

"Yes," I said.

"It's music. The most beautiful . . . is it always like this?" Dad asked, his lips hardly moving. A wreath of fireflies lit up his face.

"Sometimes," I said as softly as my breath would allow, remembering the wild boar, the deer, the dandelion fluff in Annie's hair. "Sometimes it's even more magical. When you're really still."

I felt Dad's hand on my shoulder, Laura's head leaning up against my legs, Mom's arms across my back, her hand still in mine, and Carlie warm and soft against my chest—and suddenly, for the first time in my life, I knew. I was home.

Really home.

I had made so many wishes, mostly to be left alone, to be by myself. But that wasn't what I'd needed, or at least not all of it. Deep down, I'd also needed my family around me, listening with me. To me.

Knowing who I was and loving me for it.

For a moment like this, I'd put up with a thousand hours of drums and guitars.

I had to tell them. When I did, Dad let out a broken sob. "Oh, Peter. What have I done to you?"

I'd never heard so much sadness in his voice.

"I'm sorry," I breathed. As I did, the fireflies flew up in one great cloud, circling over our heads before they fell down into the valley, a blanket of light that dispersed before it tumbled to the earth below.

"No," Mom said, pulling Dad closer and turning me to face them. "We're sorry. We never knew. Never knew this was even possible. It's so beautiful."

She clutched me to her, squishing Carlie, who mournfully protested, in the middle. "Mo dight?"

"Yes," Mom whispered. "We'll come back tomorrow and do it again. Whenever Peter wants us to come. If that's all right?"

"It's perfect," I said, grabbing her and feeling Dad wrap his arms around us all. "It's a wish come true."

It was better than anything I'd ever wished for. My life was going to be better than I'd ever dreamed, better than it ever had been—except for those days in the valley with Annie.

Annie.

If only Annie were still with me. Still in the valley. Still in the world, even. Still . . . Annie.

The sky got darker then, like a great lamp had been dimmed, and I knew I would be okay. I wouldn't run away again, wouldn't have to. But I would never be as happy as I had been. Even if everything at home changed, got perfect, Annie was gone.

And no amount of wishing would bring her back.

Chapter 30

I spent the rest of the summer making green grape jelly with Mrs. Empson, teaching Carlie how to be still enough that rabbits would come up and eat off her lap, and hugging Mom ten thousand times. She was still worried I would disappear again, I guessed. But I didn't want to run away anymore, no farther than the valley, in any case. I had everything I wanted. A friend, if I counted crazy Mrs. Empson (which I did), family, and—now that Dad had invested in some soundproofing for his music-room walls—I even had enough peace to think.

I had everything except Annie.

I'd tried to find her. Dad had even helped. We'd called MD Anderson, but they wouldn't give us any information, except that she had been a patient there. I sent a letter with photos of the art I had finished in the valley the month before school started. I'd tried to make real art, as Annie would say, but it wasn't the same. It was like the valley was asleep, after that last night when I had shown my family. That night Annie had gone away.

Maybe she had taken the magic with her. Maybe it had been her all along, bringing the magic to the place.

Maybe she had been a real wish girl after all.

I tried, though. I made forms out of cut grapevines, then waited until dark for the fireflies to come out. I took pictures of the few lightning bugs I could coax along the vines. My favorite photo was the one where the shape looked exactly like a rain lily.

I wouldn't have called my art *transformational*, but I thought Annie might have liked it. She'd probably call it *evocative*, or *phenomenological*, or some other word I'd never heard.

If she remembered words like those.

I wondered about that for a long time. Wondered if she'd recovered. If she'd had to do the treatment. If there was still any Annie left in the world, or if all that was left was what was in my heart.

There was a lot of Annie there, of course. My heart was so full of her, of memories of that week, sometimes it felt like she was there for real. When I was in the valley or sitting by Pretty Pool. Even when I saw Doug and Jake—from far away, since the police had had a talk with them and their parents about charges that might need pressing or something—I thought about Annie and how she had turned out to be the friend I hadn't known I'd needed.

The one who thought I was enough. Unique. Phenomenal.

I wished every day that she would come back. But my wishes never came true now. Annie had vanished, and she'd taken the magic with her.

And then, one day in early fall, a letter came.

There wasn't any writing, exactly. It was a picture drawn on paper that said "St. Jude's Children's Hospital" across the top.

It was hard to tell, but I thought... I thought it was a picture of damselflies covering a person—a girl who had little patches of bright red hair peeking through the insects' wings.

And at the bottom, like a title for the drawing, there were three words. The letters were all squished together and hard to read. But I was pretty sure it said: *Wish Girl, Transformed.*

My heart jumped, and I had to stop myself from shouting out loud. I grabbed the letter to my chest and ran as fast as I could to the rim of the valley. I held the page out in front of me, smiling as wide as I could. "Look," I told the valley, "look! She's alive."

Annie was alive. And making art.

And she remembered me.

Then I knew. Someday, she would come back. I knew it, like I knew how to be quiet, how to be still, how to listen. She would return to the valley and run with me through the soft thorn bushes, past the sleeping snakes, across meadows of fossils and flowers, through streams that flowed with water cleaner and purer than rain, followed by clouds of dragonflies and sparrows, butterflies and lightning bugs playing games in the sky. She would come back to us, and we would all be transformed, again and again.

I knew it. But, just to be sure, I spoke the words out loud: "I wish Annie would come back."

The breeze rushed across the branches far below, moving the brush and trees on the floor of the valley, then up the sides in strange, living green waves as it raced to me, to my ears, to answer.

Yes.

Acknowledgments

When I was a girl, I spent my summers in a Texas hill country valley that I knew was a magical place. Many moments in this book were pulled from those memories, and I thank my sister, Lari Rogge, and my mother, Rae Dollard, for their help collecting the fossils from which I built this story.

A special thanks goes to Tara Adams, oncology nurse, leukemia survivor, and friend. Thank you for reading, encouraging, and answering endless questions about your work and experience. Any medical facts I got right are thanks to you! And any factual errors, of course, are all mine. Thanks also to my brother, Dr. Ryan Loftin, for help brainstorming in the early *and* late stages—you're the best Bubba ever.

April Coldsmith graciously helped me understand some of the ways childhood leukemia can affect parent behavior and a child survivor's personality. Although I wish you hadn't had the expertise to share, April, I am so grateful you offered it.

My writer friends fill my life with magic. Thank you especially to Shelli Cornelison, Shana Burg, Shellie Faught, and Diane Collier for your critique and encouragement, and to Suzie Townsend, Danielle Barthel, and everyone at New Leaf Literary for all that and more.

Gillian Levinson has the ability to read and truly hear what I mean to say—even if it isn't on the page yet. Thank you, Gillian, for your editorial skill and friendship, and to all the amazing people at Razorbill who made my wish a reality.

And, as always, my love and gratitude belong to my very own wishes come true: Dave, Cameron, and Drew.